MW01247677

MISSING (A gripping psychological thriller with a shocking twist you won't see coming)

Ann-Marie Richards

Published by Ann-Marie Richards, 2018.

MISSING

(A gripping psychological thriller with a shocking twist you won't see coming)
by Ann-Marie Richards
Copyright 2018 by Ann-Marie Richards

ACKNOWLEDGEMENTS

Thank you Father for all my blessings. To my amazing family and friends for your love and support. Thank you Bev for your wonderful critique.

MISSING (A GRIPPING PSYCHOLOGICAL THRILLER WITH A SHOCKING TWIST YOU WON'T SEE COMING)

First edition. June 30, 2018.

Copyright © 2018 Ann-Marie Richards.

ISBN: 979-8201214104

Written by Ann-Marie Richards.

MISSING (A gripping psychological thriller with a shocking twist you won't see coming...)

Somebody was watching her every move.
They knew her schedule, where her daughter went to daycare...

After walking out of an abusive relationship, losing her job, falling into debt, and the sudden death of her parents, Isabell Morgan thought her life was beyond repair until...

She gave birth to her daughter Courtney and later found the love of her life, Erik.

Together they moved to Ocean Bay Cove, a quaint small town on the east coast, and bought an affordable fixer-upper in a cozy neighborhood. Her life seemed to be finally headed in the right direction.

And then...

Her daughter and her fiancé went missing, without a trace...

EXCERPT for Missing

Detective Luc Renald struggled to get back up on his feet, his limbs weakened and buckled under him after his eyes captured the scene before him. In all his twenty-five years on the force, he thought he'd seen everything, but *this*?

His brain was unable to process the scene before him. Trembling, he couldn't grasp the horror that befell him.

He would never look at people the same way again.

How could he?

He would never be the same again after this missing persons case. That much was true...

What baffled him more than anything was how the hell could a seasoned detective like himself have gotten it all wrong?

How did he miss the clues? The signs?

Because we all see what we want to see....

PROLOGUE

Thirty Years Ago
Newtonport, Ontario
Isabell

Eight-year-old Isabell Morgan sat with her toys lining her round Disney play table. Her favorite Cabbage Patch doll was seated across from her with a cup and saucer ready for tea.

"Okay, Mary," she called her doll, "we need to eat our breakfast so we don't get hungry."

She pretended to hear a response from her doll. "What was that? You're not hungry? But you need to eat, Mary."

She loved playing make-belief with her dolls. As an only child she always felt alone.

She tried to ignore the sounds of shouting coming from her parents' room. They always argued and shouted when they couldn't agree on something.

Her father was angry because he couldn't have any more kids. He just came back from the doctor. "Why couldn't Ken have been the one to survive?" she heard her father shout.

Ken would have been her twin brother, but he died when mommy gave birth to him. Isabell took long to come out and by the time it was his turn, he was in distress. Little did they know that sometimes Ken spoke to Isabell in her dreams. He told her he was okay where he was. Up in heaven. That's what he told Isabell.

"How's the Morgan family name going to carry on now?...She's weird. She talks to herself. She doesn't play with other kids..." her father continued on his rant.

"There's nothing wrong with her...All kids play with imaginary friends...Leave her alone..." her mother defended Isabell. Her mother always took up for her. She loved her mommy.

3

Isabell didn't mind not having lots of friends, really. The kids at school made fun of her. They called her big ears or Dumbo. They made her cry. But she didn't care. She loved her dolls. Imaginary friends didn't hurt her. They didn't say mean things about her ears or about her dress. They were nice to her.

"It's okay, Mary. I'll be fine," Isabell said as she pretended to pour tea into the empty toy cup for her doll.

"Your friend's here," she heard her mother say to her father.

"That crook? What's he doing here? I told him to stay the hell away from here."

"You'd better talk to him, Roy. He's your best friend."

"He's a crook. He's trying to weasel me out of my share. There's no way in hell I'm doing business with that jerk again."

"He wants you to buy him out."

"Hell no. He shouldn't have tried to go in on the deal without me. He's not getting a single penny more."

"We can't afford another lawsuit."

"To hell with that. He can't do squat to me. I have the goods on that guy. I know his real name. He wouldn't dare think about messing with me."

Her father never trusted anyone. He didn't like too many people. He would probably be so much happier if he played with dolls like Isabell. Dolls were not mean and they never cheated.

Isabell had placed a doll in his briefcase once, but it popped out during a meeting and all his business friends laughed at him. When he got home, mommy had to stop him from taking the belt to her. Thank God her mommy was there to protect her. Isabell was only trying to make her dad feel better.

One day, while walking home from school, Isabell couldn't help but notice a car driving slowly on the side street. Her parents told her never to talk to strangers, but this stranger was a friend of her father's. She'd seen him at the house once.

"Hi Isabell. Your parents told me to pick you up from school," the man had said to her.

Isabell's body went cold. Something was wrong. She didn't know what it was, but something was wrong. She dropped her bag and ran and ran and ran. Her heartbeat pulsed in her throat. She didn't stop until she got home safely.

Later, she'd told her parents what happened. Her father was furious, raging. Long story short, that creepy man was picked up by police at the mall for mischief. Something to do with touching a young girl at the mall. Isabell was glad she never listened to him that day. She was glad she did not get into his car. Her father had some bad friends. Since that day it was hard for Isabell to trust people. It was hard to know who to trust. That was why she liked playing with dolls—though they were only her pretend friends. They were safe. They would never hurt her.

Chapter 1

Trust your intuition. It never lies.

- Author Unknown

I watched as you got comfortable in your new home with your family. You didn't know I was watching you, but I'd been watching you for a long time now. Too long. There was a good reason, of course. I always felt you needed protecting.

You were always special. A little paranoid and unsure of yourself, but you were always special.

You're concerned about that no-name brand of smart speakers you now have in your new home—the same smart speakers you brought to Ocean Bay Cove from Newtonport.

I listened as you scolded your so-called fiancé about buying the cheaper brand instead of a well-known one from a reputable company. You wondered if anyone was listening in on your private conversations. You knew you were a little paranoid, yet you agreed with your so-called fiancé that you would keep the speakers and tell it all your worries, your schedules, your appointments, your alarm wake up times, and save all your important addresses.

Well, sometimes a little suspicion wasn't a bad thing. Such as wondering if you should avoid walking in a dark alley at night after work, or wondering why that pain in your side won't go away and if you should have it checked out. Those are healthy examples of suspicion. But the unhealthy kind would be when we turn down a good job offer because we fear we might not fit in or we don't give a relationship a try because we're afraid of being hurt. The trick was to know the difference. The trouble with you Isabell was that you don't know the difference. And that could be your downfall.

Chapter 2

Isabell

"That was so sweet of the neighbors, eh?" Isabell cuddled up with Erik on the couch in front of the Plasma TV that was mounted on one of the larger boxes. They still hadn't unpacked a lot. She didn't know when that would ever get done. It took a lot of energy and Erik had been busy with the basement.

"I can't believe Mrs. D. from next door baked cookies for Courtney, and then Dillon from down the street offered to mow our lawn until we get a lawnmower," she continued.

"Yeah, that was really nice of them. We moved to the best neighborhood." He stroked her head as she leaned into his chest. The small cast-iron fireplace, thankfully, was already in working order when they'd purchased the property. Erik had no trouble getting that started.

Her eyes darted around the living room. She hated the sight of the unpacked brown boxes but Rome wasn't built in a day. They weren't going anywhere. They'd have plenty of time to unpack the rest.

"Hello Wendi, please turn on the TV," Isabell ordered the small silver smart speakers propped on the box. At least they had that set up. It came in handy.

The smart speaker came to life. "Hello Isabell. Turning on the TV now," the disembodied female voice said.

Courtney was sound asleep in her room. She'd just been given her bath and both Erik and Isabell read from the Great Book of Fairytales to her. Erik had acted out the parts while Isabell read. They'd work so well as a mom and pop bedtime story-telling team. Erik never ceased to amaze Isabell.

"Aren't you glad we have Wendi now?" He cocked a brow.

"Very funny. I still think we should have gotten a proper one. I don't trust these cheap no-name brands. It doesn't even give you an option to turn off the speakers like the popular brands. You never know."

"Come on, we've been through that already. No one can listen in on our conversations. Besides, Wendi helped us get the listings on the best homes for sale on the East coast, remember?"

"That's true. We saved a lot of time," she agreed. "Especially after I got laid off from Ca'Andral. I don't know what I would have done."

"See. You asked Wendi to look up the nicest and most quiet neighborhoods with the lowest crime rate in the country and she delivered."

Wendi had given them great details about the town and even informed them it was going to be a seventeen-hour drive from Newtonport, a suburb just outside of Toronto, Ontario to the small quaint town of Ocean Bay Cove on the East coast of Canada in the province of Nova Scotia.

Her father brought her there once when she was much younger. He owned a few rental properties back then.

Things were more affordable in Ocean Bay Cove than the big cities. For instance, after her redundancy at her job, she and Erik could no longer afford the $2,500 a month rent in the Toronto area—which was average. And to buy a property in the hot real estate market of Toronto would cost them a fortune for an ordinary three-bedroom bungalow or semi-detached home. In Ocean Bay Cove, they got a three-bedroom, two-bathroom property of similar size right on the coast overlooking a good view of the Atlantic Ocean for just a fraction of the price.

This was a new beginning for Erik, Isabell and little Courtney.

Erik and Isabell met over a year ago in New York when she'd visited on a business trip and he'd saved her life after she had an allergic reaction to peanuts. He'd given her CPR and breathed life back into her body—and her heart.

The next thing she knew, he'd visited her in Canada a few times and that was that. Her daughter, Courtney, took an immediate liking to Erik and she hardly went to anyone. He was so cool about dating a woman who already had a child.

When Erik had asked about the father of her child, she'd admitted she'd gone to a fertility clinic, which her family wasn't even aware of. After her abusive ex, Jeff, struck her so hard she lost most of the hearing in her right ear, she found the courage to walk away. She refused, however, to give up on having children. She was already in her thirties and being a mother meant a lot to her, to have someone to raise and love. So, she decided on fertility treatment and while she technically didn't know who the father was, she was determined to give Courtney the life she deserved.

She wasn't getting any younger, being in her thirties. Being a mother meant a lot to Isabell, to have someone to raise and love.

Erik and Isabell visited Ocean Bay Cove to check it out when Isabell was still working at *Ca'Andral Department Store* —just before her layoff.

It was a good thing that Erik and she had decided to look into living in a more affordable area of the country.

The allure of a coastal getaway drew her in. As for Erik, he'd grown up in New York and LA. So he welcomed the change of pace.

Living in a big city or suburbs in the greater Toronto area wasn't exactly cheap. She didn't want to try to commute too far while having a five-year-old. Erik had just moved from the States. He'd spent time in New York City and was ready for a change. But he didn't have all his papers. He would have to wait until after they got married before he could have his social insurance number and be eligible to work in Canada.

She even got a chance to make contact with her estranged auntie. Now that her parents were deceased, she had no other close relatives. She hadn't seen her auntie in seven years. *Seven whole years.* Not a word from her. Aunt Sarah never did attend the memorial for her parents. Her phone number had changed and she'd moved from the property she'd lived in with her parents—Isabell's grandparents, until Isabell's father, Aunt Sarah's brother had taken it over and forced her out.

Aunt Sarah lived in Maine in the US so it was just a five-hour ride on the CAT ferry to Nova Scotia.

Even throughout that horrible family drama, Aunt Sarah had always been Isabell's favorite auntie.

Isabell and her aunt hadn't really spoken much. There'd been a fall out with Isabell's father, Roy and his sister, Aunt Sarah, over a will dispute over property. Ever since their parents, Isabell's grandparents had passed away, the siblings had been quarreling over the estate, the two had since fallen out. Still, she happened to see an old neighbor and family friend before leaving Newtonport who was in contact with Aunt Sarah and he gave her a current address.

Isabell sent Aunt Sarah a letter saying that she'd left Ontario and was moving to the East coast of Nova Scotia. Her aunt wrote her back and told her she was thrilled she'd made that move and would visit once she got settled in.

Isabell was settling in quickly. It wasn't hard with a nice town like Ocean Bay Cove with its well groomed farmlands, windswept lighthouses, scenic countryside, villages, rugged coastlines, serene harbors, rolling hills and evocative landscape. And adding to the natural beauty of the place a blend of old English, Spanish and French traditions and warm-hearted residents. Ocean Bay Cove was also decorated with historic buildings and sites constructed in the 18th and 19th century.

The town had an easy-going atmosphere and was known for its quiet streets, not far from the lively city where the downtown core had offbeat boutiques, restaurants and shops and plenty of galleries.

Isabell loved everything about the Victorian house they'd bought. Though it needed a lot of work, it had a beautiful green porch with peeling paint that gave it a vintage look. The windows had wooden shutters. Inside there was a cast-iron fireplace, classic details including a claw-foot tub, old wood burning stove, and Victorian era-styled banisters.

Now she could combine her love of historic homes with modern technology like having a set of smart speakers in the home.

"Okay. You're right," Isabell said, "Smart speakers are the way of the future. What am I worried about?"

"Wendi also gave us the phone number and location for the nearest daycare in our area *and* the ratings for the daycare on Yelp. She turns off the lights when we're leaving, tells us when our appointments are...She does everything. At least when I'm not here, she can keep your company and read you stuff..."

"Okay, you've got me. It's just that there's no phone customer support for that company in case anything goes wrong. And she doesn't do *everything*. It's not like we can order her to clean up the house or unpack our boxes," she grinned, cheekily.

"Very funny, Isabell," he said, his lips curved into a smile.

"Okay, fine." She sighed. "Speaking of finding nice neighborhoods, what do you think of our new neighbor Mrs. D? And what do you think she meant about making sure everyone does their part around the neighborhood?" she asked curiously.

"Baby, there's nothing to worry about. Trust me. I could see the wheels in that beautiful mind of yours spinning."

She grinned and snuggled up closer into him, his firm body felt so warm. She could feel the muscles on his ripped, chiseled chest. His heart beat strong and forceful. He was fit in every way. She was glad he'd found a gym already in the area. He'd kept trying to get her to work out with him—but she was much too shy. He always boasted he could pick her up easily since he bench-pressed two hundred pounds of iron weight when he did his weights rotation at the gym.

"You always know what's on my mind, don't you?" she said.

He pressed his soft lips to her forehead. "Hey," he said softly. "I try, beautiful. I just want you to be happy. Hey look, the folks around here seem friendly." His gaze captured hers and she felt a wave of desire coursing through her blood. What had she done to deserve such a beautiful, caring man in her life? She was thrilled to be with him. She couldn't wait to make it official once they exchanged their vows.

"That's true. They are friendly."

The scent of Erik's aftershave wafted to her nostrils. He smelled so delicious and comforting after a tiring day. He'd gone to the park with Courtney again earlier while she stayed back to unpack and wash some more dishes. There were days when she felt like going out and other days when she just wanted to settle inside.

She'd suffered with depression for years and her moods came and went. She also had a social condition called agoraphobia. She preferred not to go to public places when it was too packed, opting instead for quieter off-peak times. This had always been a challenge in taking her daughter out places. But thank God for Erik. He always stepped up to the plate.

It was he who had suggested they leave Ontario and go to the East coast to the quieter town.

Courtney and Erik were her family now.

Once they got married, he could get his papers and could start looking for work, but right now he seemed okay with fixing up their old Victorian home.

A giddy feeling surfaced in her belly as she remembered the view of the blue ocean and the boulders when they first drove to the province. It was breathtaking. She couldn't believe how close she was to the ocean. She always found it calming to be near a large body of water.

"Can't wait for Courtney to start at the Happy Dragons & Bunnies Daycare. Then I can go looking for some part-time work. I have a couple of leads."

"Anything interesting?" he asked.

"Actually, yeah. They're looking for part-time help at the local library. The hours are good. Only a few hours in the day during peak times."

"Oh good, honey," he said lovingly, rubbing her shoulders. "You always love being around books, don't you?

"Yes I do. And before I met you, they were my only escape from reality. Now I have the dream, right here beside me."

"Whatever makes you happy, sweetie." His tone was soft and reassuring. She melted into his embrace, his comforting words of acceptance.

She loved Erik. She adored everything about him. She hoped they'd be together forever. Then a sinking feeling slid inside her.

Her mind drifted to yesterday and the man she noticed staring at them from the bench at the edge of the park. He couldn't tear his eyes away from them. The man didn't smile when she'd made eye contact with him, he just continued to cast a deleterious glare in her direction. Her heartbeat sped up just thinking about it. Who was that man? Erik's back was turned at the time as he'd been playing a game of hide-and-seek with Courtney. When she did speak to Erik about it, the guy had disappeared.

"Honey?" Erik interrupted her daydream with a concerned look on his face.

Her mind drifted a lot lately.

"Thank you, baby." Her voice was quiet.

"For what?" he asked gently, his deep sexy voice penetrating her.

"For your unconditional love," she said, reaching up to him and pressing her lips to his. A sweet tingle of delight shot through her.

And...

A vibration from his pocket.

"Oh, wait a minute," Erik said, reaching for his cell phone. He glanced at the screen and his expression changed.

It was like going from warm to cold in a second.

"What's wrong?" she asked.

He looked troubled for a second then sent a text message and powered off his phone. That wasn't like him to power his phone off.

"Everything all right?"

"Yeah. Just don't want to be disturbed right now." He sighed deeply. "You know I told you about my good friend Rex out west?"

"Yeah, I remember. Is he all right?"

"Better than ever." His tone had a hint of sarcasm to it. "I'd fronted some start up money for him a while back and now that his business is doing well, he's suddenly developed a bit of amnesia. I could use those funds now. *We* could use those funds now. He forgot who helped him out to start with—and that it was a loan he'd promised to pay back."

"Oh, no. I see. Well, no worries, darling."

"I know, but I like a man who sticks to his word. Rex believes a friend in need is a friend to dodge. His answering service just left me a freaking message. I'll deal with him later."

She frowned.

"Don't worry. We'll be fine."

She was worried for more than one reason. She knew little about his "friends" and didn't like that they owed him money. What kind of business were they involved in anyway? He told her he didn't want to get into it right now whenever she probed.

She tried to divert her mind away from that line of thinking.

Erik is not Jeff. He's so much better, Isabell. Nothing to worry about.

"What's on your mind, baby?"

"A lot of things," she said, changing her train of thoughts as she gazed into the fireplace.

"Such as?"

"Courtney."

"She's a great kid. She's going to be all right."

"I know. It's just that. Well, I worry about her. She's got my ears and I'm afraid she's going to be teased."

"Your ears are beautiful."

"They're okay now. But when I was a kid, they really stuck out. I just hope the kids will be nice to her at the daycare and later when she goes to school. I don't want her to feel left out. Then there's the soother issue. I hate it when people stare at her."

"You know we'll have to wean her off it, right?"

"I know. But the doctor said she has this anxiety problem..."

"I get it but we'll have to talk about that later."

"Then we've got the bills piling up. Didn't realize the closing costs would be more than we budgeted for. I'm just worried that..."

"*Shh*, honey, we'll have enough to get by." His voice was soothing, reassuring.

"That's just it. I don't want to *just* get by. I want to have enough to pay all the bills, enjoy life and give Courtney everything she needs...I can't wait for us to get married."

She got up and reached over to one of the boxes and pulled out a large brown envelope. Though her father had given it to her just before his untimely death, the envelope was marked *Do Not Open Until September 25*, of the year they were in now.

It was odd, but her father had been odd at times. She wondered what was in the envelope, but always resisted opening it. The date was coming up soon though.

"What's that again?" Erik eyed the envelope in her hand closely.

"Something from Dad's belongings, remember? He always told me about this envelope and not to open it until September 25. Actually, he'd told my mother that if anything happened to him not to open it until then, but since they both passed away..."

"What happened to them again?"

"Carbon monoxide poisoning or so they'd suspected."

"Why do you say that?"

It was hard to explain this sixth sense feeling in her gut that told her it wasn't an accident—only made to look like one.

The case was still under investigation as her father had always been involved in nefarious activities and during that time he'd been arguing with some business partners about an online scam. Something had gone horribly wrong. Her mother had warned him about it, but he didn't listen. She was used to it, unfortunately, since he hadn't exactly been on the clean side of things throughout their marriage. Isabell always hated that he was constantly getting involved in something shady. Yet, he was a loving father to his family. At least, that was what she believed.

"Oh, nothing. The case is closed. Anyway, I'm so sorry you never got a chance to meet them. They would have liked you." Erik had met her a month before they had died—just over a year ago. But he never got the chance to visit Canada until after their deaths.

"I'm sure I would have liked them too." He hesitated for a moment. "Do you think there are some bonds or something in that envelope?"

"Who knows? He did say something about how I would never have to worry about money again. Not sure why he would want it to be opened at a certain date though."

"Is it some kind of superstition thing?"

"Not sure. He just warned that it's important to not open it before this date or something bad might happen." She sighed.

"Something bad? Like what?"

She shrugged. "Dad was always secretive *and* paranoid."

"Paranoid?"

She didn't want to tell Erik too much. "Yeah, he sometimes had this paranoia. He felt if he told people too much, they'd try to...I don't know, let's just say he watched way too many murder mysteries involving heirs." She shook her head and grinned. "Anyway, I doubt it's anything useful."

She placed it down on the side table. Her dad was terrible with money and always squandering it away. She just couldn't see him leaving her anything of value that he wouldn't take for himself, especially considering how far in debt he was when he passed. The money she had in the bank would only last them so long, especially with the insane daycare costs. It almost worked out to be the same as she would be bringing in, but it would be better for Courtney to mingle with other kids and Isabell wanted to go out and work. A part time job to keep up her office skills was all she needed for now.

"As soon as you get your papers you can start working in Canada."

"I know. Trust me, I'm not used to just sitting at home."

"Or going to the gym so often," she playfully teased him.

"Cheeky."

"What? Believe me, I'm glad you hang out there. I'm loving the results." She purred.

He grinned and playfully rolled his eyes. "Glad you love the results."

She knew it bothered him that he couldn't provide for his family. He was laid off two years ago from a software company then began his own online start-up that, unfortunately, went bust. He also tried some other ventures with former associates of his that went nowhere. He grew up in a rough neighborhood and tried to keep his nose clean, he'd told her but he needed to work and keep on things. It wasn't easy.

"You're trembling, baby," he said as he held her.

"I'm fine. I'll be...fine," she said, feeling a sense of uneasiness.

Chapter 3

The reception wasn't clear as I tried to listen in on your conversation. We all have a right to feel safe in our own homes, speaking freely about anything without fear of having our privacy invaded—but trust me, I was doing it for your own good.

As I struggled to listen in, I noticed the unease in your voice. I wish you would listen to your instincts. Trust your intuition

You clearly had no idea your conversations with your so-called fiancé were being carefully monitored. No clue.

You made it so much easier to do what I have to do. You carefully planned out everything to the last detail. So did I. We have a lot in common, don't we? More than you could ever know.

Your wounds go deeper than I could have possibly imagined as I listen to you talk to your so-called fiancé. Your perfect love. A man you're convinced would never hurt you like your ex did because Erik was different. Well, you were right about one thing. Erik was unlike any other man you'd dated.

Isabell Morgan, I wish you could open your eyes and really see the truth.

Chapter 4

Isabell

Later, Erik came into the bathroom and wrapped his arms around Isabell's waist. She leaned back into his firm muscular chest.

"You're the best thing that's ever happened to me," he whispered into her good ear. The scent of his cologne wafted to her nose. He smelled as good as he felt.

What had she done to deserve such a handsome, caring partner? Her soon to be husband.

She glanced into the mirror. They made a beautiful couple, didn't they? Some would say the perfect couple. In every way.

She turned around to look into his beautiful mahogany-grey eyes. "I love you," she said.

"Love you more, baby," he whispered to her and brushed his sweet lips against hers.

"You're the most beautiful woman in the world. I'm so lucky to have you. Isabell, I'm going to take such great care of you and Courtney. You'll never want for anything." His words were reassuring, comforting to her. His deep mellow voice sent shivers of delight running down her back.

Her lips couldn't help but curve into an appreciative smile.

Erik was so different from Jeff, her ex-boyfriend. Worlds apart.

She ended up with Jeff because abusive treatment was all she knew. Erik was nicer though. Agreeable.

Though there were times when she wondered if she was missing something, such as maybe Erik was like Jeff, only he managed to hide it better. She pushed that crazy idea out of her mind.

Erik was a good man.

She thought men who knew how to treat a lady only existed in romance novels. But he was her hero - and he was all hers. Soon she would officially become Mrs. Erik Joneson and she couldn't wait.

After losing her parents so tragically, she thought she'd lost her family. Now she had Courtney and Erik.

The following morning...

Isabella yawned as she made her way out of the bedroom into the bathroom down the hall, the floorboards squeaking with every step. Erik left his jacket haphazardly hanging on the top of the stairs. The hallway was scattered with plush toys, dried toast crusts and a juice stain. What the heck? She'd just cleaned the floor yesterday. Courtney was sound asleep right now so she must have spilled the juice on the ground last night

Isabell grinned.

"Oh, well. Most people might get upset about a messy house where toys are strewn about, crumbs are left on the ground, and dirty clothes overflowed from baskets, but what it all means is that at least I have a family—and for that I am thankful for. At least I have kid to clean up after, and a partner who's there for me," she said to herself.

A messy floor meant she was living in a home with her family. A safe place. It was all hers.

Don't complain about the problems you have, be thankful for the ones you don't have, she remembered reading somewhere.

Life was one big beautiful mess, an obstacle course filled with challenges to overcome, an adventure to be explored, not a linear line of neatness and boredom. We all needed challenges. Life was full of surprises. She would take that any day.

After she got ready for the day, she headed downstairs where the scent of bacon and eggs lured her to the kitchen.

Her smile widened.

The kitchen looked as if a hurricane had whooshed through. Erik was a good cook, but not the neatest in the world.

"Baby, you've made breakfast again? I told you it was my turn," she said, playfully.

"No, no. You rest your pretty little self and let me do all the cooking. Besides, until I get another job, I don't mind doing all the work around here."

"Aww. But then what does that leave me with?"

"Taking care of yourself. Practice yoga. Isabell, you've been through hell and back these past years. I still want to rip that guy apart for what he did to you." He leaned down, sorrow in his eyes as he stroked her disfigured earlobe before he gently pressed his lips to it.

She felt hot inside, then an indescribable feeling. What was that feeling?

"It's okay. It's in the past," she said.

"He should have spent more time in prison."

"But he didn't, so it's okay." She didn't want to discuss it further. Jeff came from money so his daddy somehow worked the system and made sure he got less time served.

Jeff had emotionally and physically abused her. He'd told her she was worthless. He'd used her illness against her with intimidation and manipulation, trying to completely control her. He'd told her that no other man could have her if she left him. He'd put so much fear into her she thought she'd never recover. However, she refused to let his words intimidate her forever and found the courage to leave Jeff. She'd packed her bags and was ready to run out into the night. That was when he stopped her. That was when he struck the first blow.

She squeezed her eyes shut.

"What's wrong, baby?" Erik said gently, concern in his deep voice.

"It's nothing." Isabell wiped the memory from her mind.

She was not about to let her ex steal her joy by remembering the horror of the past. She had Erik now. And he and Courtney were her future

"I'm going to wake up Courtney," she said.

"No, I'll do that, beautiful."

He left and she'd heard him go into Courtney's room and turn on the light. "Rise and shine, princess," he said.

"Morning, Daddy," she said back.

Isabell looked into the magnetic mirror pinned on the fridge door. What did she see? A woman who'd been so badly damaged she didn't think she could ever have a future that was hopeful.

Now that she had it, would that sinking feeling that it was all about to end ever go away?

She couldn't help but to wonder if Jeff would ever try to make good on his promise—his threat.

Later, after breakfast, she walked up the old wooden staircase. The floorboards creaked like crazy. Erik said he would go up to the hardware store and get something to fix the loud noise. She didn't know how he was going to do that exactly.

As she walked along the landing, she glanced out the small window to the backyard and thought she saw a man in a dark outfit standing there.

Isabell screamed.

"What is it, baby?" Erik called out from the kitchen.

When she looked again, there was no one there. Was her mind playing cruel tricks on her?

She could have sworn she saw someone.

"Baby, what is it?" Erik raced up the steps to Isabell's side. She probably looked as if she was paralyzed with fear. Well that was how she felt.

"I...I think I saw someone."

He spun around and went to the window. "There's no one there, sweetie."

She swallowed hard.

"Are you sure?" he asked.

She went over to the window. "Someone was...watching us, Erik. I...I just don't feel comfortable." *Someone was watching us, just like that man at the park.*

"Listen, wait here." Erik rushed back downstairs, two steps at a time, then he grabbed his other jacket and opened the back door and went outside.

A few moments later, he was back inside.

"Did you see anyone?" Isabell hugged herself, still frozen to the spot in the middle of the winding stairwell.

"No, I didn't."

She rubbed her arms.

"What is it, Isabell?" Erik's tone was gentle. So gentle, she immediately felt calmer. He was so patient with her. He took her background, social anxieties and agoraphobia all in stride and always treated her with such tender care. He was perfect in every way. He understood her and stood by her. He never thought she was crazy, like her ex. This truly was unconditional love.

"Mommy, are you okay?" the little precious voice of her baby girl sounded. Courtney stood at the top of the steps with her plush toy in her hand. She then held onto the rail and climbed down the steps toward her.

"Yes, Mommy's fine, baby." She stroked Courtney's curly locks.

When she glanced up she saw a man again outside the window and screamed.

Erik ran back up the steps.

The man had disappeared.

Low fences surrounded the backyard. There was a broken section in the fence so anyone could scoot over from the other backyards. There was an abandoned house down the road. Did the person come through that house? She refused to believe it could have been one of the neighbors.

Erik went back outside to look around while she and Courtney headed downstairs to wait for him. When he came back inside, he shook his head.

"Are you sure you weren't seeing things, sweetie? There's a tall shrub over the other side. It looks like it could be a person, but it isn't."

Isabell shivered uncontrollably, hugging herself.

"Oh, baby. You really do believe you saw someone. I'm calling the police," he said.

"No. No. Please don't. Maybe it was my overactive imagination," she said.

"Are you sure?"

She nodded. "Erik, my daddy was very paranoid. He also suffered from...well, anyway...I think it runs in the family." Something else ran in the family too. She wished she could tell Erik but then he might change his mind about her and disappear out of her life—her heart.

Erik listened attentively, rubbing her shoulders. "It doesn't have to run in the family, sweetie."

"I know. But...there's more. My dad wasn't always on the straight and narrow. He and my mom always argued about his business ventures. He would lock all doors and tell me not to trust people. He said people were after him. Their deaths might have been ruled as an accident, but I believe..."

"Shh, it's all right, sweetie," he whispered to her.

They both looked at Courtney who was, thankfully, in a world of her own watching a cartoon on TV.

"It's all right," Erik said again.

"Maybe you're right. Maybe I was just seeing things." She didn't want to alarm him. But her gut was telling her otherwise.

She wanted to believe that everything would be all right. She really did. But she had a sinking feeling that reality and delusions were beginning to blur into a thin line, a line she was afraid she wouldn't be able to cross.

Uneasiness swept over her, leaving her cold.

Whether it was all in her mind or not...Someone. Was. Watching. Them.

Chapter 5

Not everyone was familiar with the term Neighborhood Watch. What did it really mean? It meant that people looked out for each other. And they did. I am about to help you out of your misery. Make your life so much more easier without you realizing it. You really need help, Isabell.

Neighborhood Watch meant that people were watching, not just the going ins and going outs, but they were watching you. Your movements. How many friends you have visiting you. They made judgments about you without even realizing it.

Your business. People were people watchers and judgers by nature. But what did that mean?

It meant that you needed to be aware. It meant that people sometimes pretended to be what was expected of them. As I watched you, I realized you were pretending to be what everyone wanted you to be. You were pretending to be what you thought you should be.

The pretense needed to come to an end now.

I had no idea you would even be home at that time. I thought the home would be empty.

I'd been looking up some information about you online.

You didn't know what was real and what wasn't.

I flung the binoculars across the bed and picked up the phone to make a call.

"Yeah," the man answered on the other end of the line.

"Slight change in plans."

"What d'ya mean?"

"Hold off."

"The retainer fee is the same." The voice was cold and forceful.

"Trust me, you'll get what's coming to you."

The man on the other end of the phone line hung up without saying anything else.

Don't worry, Isabell. I won't harm you. I think I know how to get what I want without hurting you.

Chapter 6

Isabell

Later that evening, Isabell went into her daughter's room and opened the door slightly.

Her heart melted as she saw her little girl snuggled up under the sheets holding onto her plush toy fast asleep. She looked so adorable with her long eyelashes resting on her cheeks. She really did look like her mommy, didn't she?

The little night-light was on in the corner. Courtney was always afraid of the dark and Isabell wanted to make sure she'd never wake up in the night thinking she saw monsters. Courtney had trouble sleeping sometimes. One night she screamed out and Erik bolted out of the bed first and they both ran into Courtney's room and turned on the light. Erik had grabbed the bat that was in the corner, ready to strike the intruder.

"Mommy, there's a monster."

They didn't see anyone else.

"A monster? Where baby?"

"At the window. Outside."

Erik immediately went to the window, the baseball bat he kept in the corner of our room in his hand, and pulled back the sheer curtain and looked outside. They hadn't been able to afford blinds yet so the curtains that could easily be seen through were the window's only coverage.

"I don't see anything, sweetie." His voice was calm and reassuring yet his eyebrows furrowed with concern.

Courtney jumped out of the bed and grabbed her plush toy to her chest. "I'm scared, Mommy."

Isabell's heart pounded fiercely in her chest. "It's all right, baby. It's going to be okay." She hugged Courtney to her chest.

"What if the monster comes back?" Courtney said.

"I'm going outside to check around the back," Erik had said.

"You sure, honey?" Isabel asked, wondering if it was the same guy she thought she saw before.

It was late at night. She worried about Erik going outside in the dark.

"Yeah." He went into the bedroom and pulled on his pants over his pajama bottoms.

Isabell continued to hug her daughter to her chest while Erik hurried down the wooden staircase and to the back door.

Isabell encouraged Courtney to get back to bed and then sang her a lullaby until she went to sleep.

It had been a good ten minutes later and Erik still hadn't returned. Isabell covered Courtney with the Princess bed cover and turned off the light, leaving the nightlight on. She then went looking for Erik.

"Erik," she called out. There was no one.

Isabell made her way down the wooden staircase, her steps making a clunking sound on the hardwood. She went outside in her dressing gown, wrapping the robe straps around her waist.

"Erik," she called out again, her heart palpitating hard in her chest. The hairs on the back of her neck stood up.

What if there was an intruder? What if he got to Erik?

"Oh my God," she cried out, as a hand landed on her shoulder. She spun around and saw it was Erik.

"You scared me," she said.

"Sorry about that," he said in a low voice.

"Did you see anything? Or anyone?"

"No. Nothing." He glanced around in the dark, his flashlight in his hand.

Just then a light from one of the neighbors turned on in the upstairs room. A woman stood at the window staring out at them.

Isabell hugged herself. The neighbors probably thought they were up to something.

Erik looked up at the window. The shadow of the woman seemed to look back before she drew the drapes. The light in her room then went out.

Mrs. D. That had to be Mrs. D.

Erik hugged Isabell and led her back inside the house.

When they went back inside the house Isabell went to check on Courtney. Panic rose in her chest. Her eyes widened in shock. She screamed out.

Erik rushed beside her. "What is it baby?"

"Courtney!" she shouted, looking at the empty bed with the sheets pulled back.

She was gone from her room.

Why the hell did Isabell leave to go outside to look for Erik?

Erik then went to their own room and he said, "It's okay, she's in here."

Isabell went to his side and saw Courtney cuddled up on their bed. A sigh of relief escaped her lips as her muscles relaxed again. There went her overactive imagination again.

There went her overactive imagination again.

Yes, her overactive imagination. She'd been told she had one ever since she was a child. She could dream up anything. Did Courtney take after her? Did she imagine seeing someone at the window? But then he would have had to be on some serious 8-foot stilts like those circus performers or somehow climbed up a ladder since Courtney's room was up on the second floor.

They took Courtney back into her own room and she snuggled on the bed beside her daughter while Erik lay on the floor. By 2 o'clock in the morning everything was quiet and they returned to their room.

What a night it had been. If only they'd known that was only the beginning of many crazy nights. That was nothing compared to what was to happen to them in the coming days.

Chapter 7

Isabell

The following morning, when Isabell went downstairs she saw Erik standing by the window in the living room on his cell phone.

He was speaking in a low, whispered voice so she could hardly hear what he was saying.

Don't be paranoid, Isabell. He's a good man. Erik's nothing like Jeff.

"Everything all right?" she asked him, concerned.

He spun around, a stunned expression on his face. "Oh, sweetie, how long have you been standing there?"

How long have I been standing there?

Not how are you doing? Or good morning, but how long have you been standing there? Which translated to how much did you hear, didn't it?

Her thoughts flashed back to Jeff, who'd been talking to his mistress in a low voice once. She'd caught him. She told him she was moving out. That's when he'd gone crazy on her. Their relationship had gone downhill from there.

Calm your thoughts, Isabell. Stop being so overdramatic. That was the past. Don't let Jeff ruin your happiness with another man. All men are not the same. Erik is different.

Erik *was* different, she told herself. He was a good man.

She made a conscious decision to stop looking for faults. Whatever you seek you will find.

We all see what we want to see...

She knew that all too well. Jeff had been a cheater all his life and all he knew were women who cheated like him. She was different yet He didn't see that she was different. He'd assume that whenever she was with her friends or visiting her parents that she was really with another guy. He was a crazy paranoid lover who was doing the very thing he'd wrongfully accused her of.

31

Trust.

She needed to trust that Erik wasn't going to break her heart like Jeff did.

"Oh I just got here," she said, concern knitting her brows.

He looked relieved. "Oh, good."

Oh, good?

"Breakfast is ready." He turned off the phone and slid it in his jeans pocket as headed into the kitchen. "You want to go into town around two o'clock?" he asked, dividing bacon and eggs into three plates.

"No, it's okay. It's going to be busy in the town later. Why not the park nearby?"

A shadow of disappointment slid across his handsome face. They hadn't really been out much since moving to Ocean Bay Cove. She felt a sense of guilt that she was taking away his joy. No wonder he spent a lot of time at the gym. It was bad enough he didn't have his papers to legally work yet, or even seek employment. She hoped he'd understand though.

"Sure." His clipped tone resonated with disappointment.

As if sensing her apprehension he told her whom he was talking to on the phone.

"By the way," he said. "I was just talking to my buddy out west."

"Yes, what did he have to say?"

He sighed deeply. "Remember I told you I loaned him some money and he was supposed to send it back to me from one of his business deals?"

"Oh, I see." She didn't sound too convinced. She tried not to think about it.

"Mommy," Isabell heard her daughter's tiny voice called out.

She left the kitchen and hurried upstairs to go and get her daughter.

"Hi sweetie, you just woke up?"

"Yes mommy," she said as she rubbed her eyes and held onto her plush toy.

Isabell went to the side of the bed and looked out the window and thought she saw a shadow. She squinted to get a closer look. It was gone. No one was there. Nothing was there.

Was her mind playing tricks on her again?

Why did this whole town seem so creepy all of a sudden?

Why was everything seemingly so...odd?

Stop looking out the window, Isabell.

She swallowed hard. Then she felt her daughter's hand in her own.

Then everything seemed okay again and she hugged her daughter close to her.

Maybe Isabell needed to get back on her medication. A month after her parents' death she'd weaned herself off her meds, but right now she wished she were back on them. They kept her calm, at least. Her father never believed in doctors or medicine.

But that didn't help *him* much.

She sighed deeply.

One day at a time. One thought at a time.

"Come, let's get ready. Daddy's made breakfast for us and later we can go to the park."

"Okay, Mommy."

Just then she heard the loud banging sound of the pipes in the kitchen downstairs, yet another house repair needed. Erik insisted he could fix the pipes himself and they'd save a ton of money instead of hiring a plumber. But Isabell wondered if that was a critical mistake.

"Hey baby, I'm just going to stop by the hardware store to get some duct tape for the pipe. It's just a temporary fix until we figure out what's going on," he said as she and Courtney came down the stairs.

"Oh, um...okay. Courtney and I will head to the park alone. We'll be fine."

"You sure?"

"Sure. The forecast calls for rain in the afternoon anyway. So I'll take Courtney right after breakfast. It should be nice now, I don't think there'll be any crowds. The park's just five minutes walk from here." Not like in the town where it would be crowded and a good half hour from their home. She swallowed hard. He walked over to her and pressed his sweet lips to her forehead.

"Why don't you wait until I get back? I'll take you to the park."

"No, Erik. You go. We'll be fine. I'd rather not go later because there'll be more people at the park."

"Right," he said in a low voice. "Fine. I'll catch up with you guys later, all right? Want me to pick up lunch?"

"Sure. That would be great."

"McDonalds!" Courtney belted out.

They both grinned.

"Maybe you should have carrots and..." Isabell offered.

Courtney wrinkled her nose. "No. McDonald's," she persisted.

"Hey no worries. You can have McDonald's at lunch and a nutritious dinner later. How's that?" Erik said.

"Yay! McDonald's."

They both grinned and shook their heads. It was such a pleasure having a sweet little angel in their life and Erik was a wonderful father figure. She couldn't believe how much she'd lucked out. She really couldn't believe it. She just hoped and prayed her perfect world would not come crumbling down as it had in the past.

She drew in a deep breath then proceeded to get Courtney dressed for the day.

"Wendi, what's the forecast for today?" Erik asked.

The smart speaker was silent. The light was on but it didn't respond.

"Wendi? Hello? Is it going to rain in the afternoon or the evening?" Isabell asked.

"The forecast for Ocean Bay Cove calls for light showers around four o'clock," the disembodied voice sounded.

"Thanks, Wendi," Isabell said annoyed. "I guess she only speaks when she's in the mood. I knew we should have gotten a smart speaker from a reputable company. I don't feel good about that thing."

'I'm sure she's fine. Just like you'll be."

Isabell started to hyperventilate.

"Baby, you're having another panic attack. Take a deep breath. It's just a set of speakers. Glitches happen all the time. Try to relax before you go to the park."

She drew in a deep breath.

Everything will be okay, she tried to convince herself. Though there was a shadow of doubt cast across her mind right now. She had a sinking feeling that something was wrong but she couldn't quite put her finger on it. Not yet, anyway...

Chapter 8

As I powered on my laptop, I waited for the home screen to appear. I went into a search browser to look up information about your illness.

I needed to educate myself as much as possible on your rare condition. You really needed to take a deep breath.

Relax.

You would need all the strength you could get for what you were about to deal with later.

Chapter 9

Isabell

An hour later, Isabell took Erik's advice to take a deep breath and relax before going to the park with Courtney. She stepped onto the porch, glancing around. She drew in a breath of fresh country air. Now this was the life. The birds were chirping in the distance. She could feel the warmth of the sun on her face and the gentle breeze on her neck. No sound of traffic or sirens. The neighborhood had a relaxed aura to it. It was a picture perfect neighborhood. Everyone took pride in their homes. The hedges were all neatly trimmed; all the lawns were mowed. The porches were freshly painted on Garden Green Blvd. Except for the number 47 fixer upper they were currently living in, of course. But that would change soon. Erik said he'd get around to doing that as soon as he fixed a few things inside the house.

As long as everyone does their part...we wouldn't want the property values to go down.

Mrs. Donigan's words echoed in Isabell's mind. A sudden chill slid over her. Then out of the corner of her eye, she noticed a figure watching her from the fence next door and jumped.

It was Mrs. Donigan, standing behind her white picket fence looking over.

"Oh, hi Mrs. D. Um...I didn't see you there." She sure was quiet. How long had she been standing there? She wasn't there when Isabell first came outside.

If Mrs. D. ever needed a part-time gig in retirement she could always work as a cat burglar. No one would ever hear her coming.

Though Mrs. Donigan was one of the first to introduce herself, she was a bit strange. Nice lady though. She had the worse eyesight on the planet, Isabell thought to herself.

"Hi there," Mrs. D. said then turned around. "Here Missy, Missy," Mrs. D. called out looking troubled.

"Is everything all right, Mrs. D?"

"I can't find my pussy."

"Excuse me?"

"My little pussy cat. My kitty cat."

"Oh, right. Of course. What does she look like?"

"She has bushy black fur."

"A black cat. I see."

"Where?"

"No. What I mean is, I'll look out for her."

Isabell went out looking for her kitty in the near bushes. "Where do you think she went? Has she been out before?"

"Not really."

Later, Mrs. D. shouted from the back that she'd found her. She had a ball of fur huddled to her chest.

"Mrs. D!" Isabell's eyes widened.

"What is it, dear?"

"Good God! That's a...a raccoon!"

The raccoon wiggled wildly then leaped out of her arms and scattered away. She should be lucky she wasn't bitten or scratched by the wild animal.

"Oh dear." Mrs. D frowned.

"Mrs. D. Don't you wear glasses?" She noticed she had them on the other day when she greeted them and introduced herself.

"I do. But I can't seem to find them, dear."

"Oh, no."

Isabell stepped down from her porch and went to the woman's home and helped her find them.

Poor thing had taken them off to have a bath, according to what she'd said, and left them on the counter and couldn't find them. Isabell wondered how Mrs. D managed everyday.

"There they are," Isabell said, picking up the glasses from the counter.

"Oh, thank you so much, dear."

"Um...Mrs. D. isn't that your cat," she said, pointing to the area by the fireplace. The little black kitty was curled up in a ball in her kitty basket.

"Oh, dear." She moved closer. "Yes, dear. You're right."

Okay.

Isabell chuckled. "Are you all right?"

"I was just remembering about the time when I mixed up my husband Bert's medicine."

"Oh?"

"He suffered from Arthritis."

Suffered? Or suffers?

"I went to give him his night time medicine and it turned out to be my water pill." She giggled. "Poor thing was up all night going to the bathroom."

"Oh no."

"Oh yes, dear. Then of course, our daughter insisted since then that she would do everything for him. Oh, well. They're together *now.*"

There was strangeness to her tone of voice.

Isabell wondered if Mrs. D had accidentally given her husband the wrong medicine because she couldn't see well. Unfortunately, it looked as if pride was an issue for her too. She probably didn't want to think of herself as helpless.

Isabell noticed the door leading to the basement was bolted with a bar across it. She couldn't imagine why she needed that in this nice quiet neighborhood. Was she afraid of someone breaking in? She supposed it didn't hurt to be extra cautious since she was an older lady living alone.

"Well, I'd better be going now. I'm taking Courtney to the park soon."

"Oh, isn't that lovely. I wish I still had a daughter to take to the park."

A strange feeling befell Isabell but she shrugged it off. She turned to leave and noticed the kitten by the fireplace had a tag on its tail. When she looked closer she almost gasped. It was a price tag. The kitty was one of those realistic looking plush pets.

It was a toy, not a real living pet.

* * *

"What's so strange about that?" Erik said to Isabell later while he fixed the pipes underneath the kitchen sink. "Can you hand me the wrench, babe?"

"Sure." She reached over and handed him the tool.

"I just think she's a sweet lady, but she really needs help. I mean she pretends the cat is real."

"Well, maybe to her it is. Remember, she's all alone and it doesn't look as if her old man or daughter call her."

Isabell wondered if they were even alive.

Stop that, Isabell. Calm your overactive imagination down.

She wondered why the basement door was bolted shut. And what was with that steel bar across it?

Chapter 10

Isabell

"Darling, why don't you go and play with the other kids," Isabell said, feeling sorry for her daughter.

Courtney shook her head. She covered her ears with her hat as much as she could. She held onto to her little book and plush toy in the other hand. Her ears peaked through the hat as it pulled up again. Not a big deal. In Isabell's mind, her daughter had beautiful ears. She was perfect. But unfortunately, she knew not everyone would see it that way. Oftentimes people would stare at her in the supermarket when Isabell sat her in the kid seat of the shopping cart. They would look at her ears and laugh.

Well, too bad for them. Isabell felt like saying something but often held her tongue.

"I don't want you to be lonely, sweetie."

"I'm not lonely, Mama. Look, she held up her plush toy in her hand. "I have my friend, Becky." Courtney smiled with her two front teeth missing. She looked positively adorable.

Isabell's heart melted as an aching feeling rushed through her. Courtney reminded Isabell of when she was young. Her toys were her only friends too. But she wanted Courtney to have a normal life socializing with other kids too.

She could see off into the distance some kids were playing on the slides at the park. A few of the older ones were staring at the screens on their smartphones.

"Okay, sweetie." Isabell swallowed hard. She noticed a girl stopped and looked at Courtney and laughed. She nudged another kid and they both burst out laughing. Someone called out and said something about big ears and Dumbo and bat ears.

Courtney held her head down.

Isabell's heart squeezed inside her chest. "It's okay, sweetie. Come on. Let's go get some ice cream."

"Okay."

She got up from the park bench and held onto her daughter's hand as they headed back to the exit area of the Ocean Bay Community Park.

It was starting to drizzle with rain now so it was good timing. Besides, her hay fever was beginning to act up now. She didn't like being outdoors too much. She didn't like when people stared at her and her little girl.

Chapter 11

Isabell

That night, Isabell slept fitfully. She had three dreams. She remembered them distinctly. In the first dream, her ex had been drinking; he chased her around the apartment. She left. In the second dream, she'd found her parents dead. Then in the third dream, she was lying in a hospital bed with the steel side rails up. That dream didn't make any sense. The first two happened, but the last dream was horrible. The nurse came into the room with her newborn baby and handed her little bundle of joy to her, only when she pulled back the newborn blanket, there was nothing there.

Isabell screamed out.

"Honey, are you all right?" Erik got up and turned on the bedside lamp.

Isabell broke out into a sweat, panting, trying to catch her breath. "Sorry, I...I had a horrible dream." She explained the dreams to him.

"It's okay, baby," he said, holding her tight. The scent of his cologne wafted to her nostrils, his strong warm body on hers comforted her.

"Thank you," she said, softly.

"It's all right." His voice was calm and reassuring.

"I'm worried, Erik. I'm worried about Courtney. Why was the baby blanket empty?"

"It's all right, baby. It was just a dream. Sometimes dreams don't make any sense. It's just random thoughts from stuff we think about. Not necessarily a premonition or anything."

She sighed deeply. She felt stuffy again and reached for a tissue to blow her nose.

"Your sinuses acting up again?" he asked gently.

"Yeah. You know how it is this time of the year. I think I might be catching a cold too."

"You want me to make you anything? Some warm honey and lemon?"

"No. I'll be fine, thanks. Let's just get back to sleep."

He hugged her after he turned off the bedside lamp. They were in darkness again. She glanced out at the moonlight coming through the thin drapes. Would she ever come out of the darkness in her mind?

Chapter 12

Isabell

Isabell didn't feel up to going to the park today. Erik had taken Courtney and said he'd be back soon. She made her way down the wooden staircase to the kitchen and glanced out the window at the garden. The sky was a bit overcast. It would probably start raining soon. She hoped they wouldn't be too long.

Isabell's stomach tightened into little knots. There was that feeling again.

She tried to convince herself that it was all in her mind. A lot of things were all in her mind. Why oh, why did she have that sinking feeling? She walked over to the kitchen and picked up the phone to dial Erik's cell phone.

"Hey," he answered.

She breathed a sigh of relief. "Oh, thank God."

"What's wrong? Are you okay?"

"Oh it's nothing. I was just worried about you guys. Will you be home soon? Looks like it's going to rain."

"Yeah, we're on our way. Courtney made a few friends."

Her heart leaped in her chest. "Really? At the park?" The other day, the kids were so mean to her. She couldn't believe she'd finally found some nice friends.

"Yeah, this nice old couple..."

Isabell's heart sank. "Oh, that's nice."

"What's wrong?" He sounded a bit breathy as if he was walking briskly while talking.

"Nothing. I just hope Courtney can find some friends her own age, too. That's all."

"Listen, there's nothing to worry about, sweetie. She'll be fine when she starts daycare."

"I hope so."

"Isabell, relax."

"Okay," she finally agreed.

When they finished off the phone, Isabell looked at the wooden door leading to the basement. It was slightly ajar. Did Erik leave it open?

She walked over to close it then noticed the light was on downstairs. Erik probably left it on when he was working on fixing the steps. She knew he'd be back soon but she didn't want to run up the light bill or waste energy. They were, after all, on a tight budget.

Isabell made her way down the steps to turn off the light when one of the lower steps gave out and her foot went through it. Her ankle twisted and she let out a scream in pain.

Oh, no. Agony coursed through her body. She was going to die there if Erik didn't find her in time.

She sat there, unable to get up, for what seemed like hours when she noticed a man walking by the side of the house through the small basement windows. She didn't recognize the shoes or the pants. Who was it?

Fear kept her frozen while she lay helpless at the bottom of the steps. She hoped and prayed he would not squat down and look through the windows and see her in this vulnerable position.

Who was it? Was someone watching her? If he wanted to see her, wouldn't he just knock on the door? Her eyes followed as the man walked around to the other side, then...

He vanished.

Isabell let out a breath, her pulse pounded in her throat. Someone was watching her. Someone was watching their house.

* * *

"Baby, what were you doing down there?" Erik said later, bandaging her ankle. He seemed more annoyed than anything.

"Someone was watching our house, Erik. Someone was outside. A man."

"Are you sure?"

"Yes. I'm sure?"

"Sure it wasn't the mail guy?"

"I'm sure. He didn't deliver any letters. It was as if he was checking to see if there was an open door or..."

Isabell realized how foolish she sounded.

"Listen. I'll check that out, but in the meantime you'll need to keep off your feet for a while."

"I'll be fine, really."

"No, you won't, sweetie. Not if you bear weight on this thing."

"It's just a little sprain."

He leaned down and kissed her ankle. "It's all right."

"Mommy, are you going to be okay?" Courtney said, holding on to her little plush toy.

"Of course, sweetie." Isabell stroked her hair. "Of course."

"Okay." Her tiny voice was so cute. She ran off with her plush toy into the living room to watch the Disney channel as if without a care in the world. That was the way it should be for a little girl. The worrying should be left up to the parents.

Boy, did Isabell have enough to last a lifetime. She truly believed she'd be still worrying over Courtney even after she graduated college and got married and had kids of her own. Parents never stopped worrying did they?

"Listen, I'll take Isabell on her first day to the daycare," Erik said. "No need to worry, all right?"

"Are you sure?"

"Yes. Between your cold and your sprained ankle, you're in no condition to be trotting down the street. You can take her when you're feeling better. Besides, it's not like I have work right now."

"I know."

He had a point, but she was gutted that she wouldn't be taking Isabell on her first day at the daycare. She wanted to see how Courtney reacted to the new environment.

"It'll be all right, Isabell," she told herself, though she really didn't feel that way.

Chapter 13

Isabell

The next day, Isabell watched as Erik walked with Courtney down the street into the fog-filled morning. He waved to her and blew her a kiss. She waved back through the screen door. Courtney turned around and waved to her mother and Isabell blew another kiss to her and waved back. "See you soon, sweetie," she said.

Courtney glanced back again and Isabell's heart squeezed in her chest. She missed her little girl already. She knew that she had to go to daycare, but she was worried about her being the new kid. Would she make new friends today?

Oh, God. Would the kids be kind to her, given her...unique appearance? Isabell's gut twisted thinking about that.

She's a child, Isabell. She's resilient. All children are resilient, remember?

Her mother's words came back like a haunted whisper. Her mother had always been right. She missed her parents more and more every day.

She sighed deeply. Her gaze shifted across the street. She thought she saw the curtain move from the neighbor's window. Was someone watching her?

She'd heard of the neighborhood watch, but man did this street give her the creeps.

Suddenly, a feeling of dread wrapped around her. She worried about her daughter and her fiancé. A wild thought blew into her mind. What if someone was out to get them?

But that was crazy. She had to sweep those paranoid thoughts out of her head. This was a new town, a new chance at life.

No one knows about your past, Isabell. You're safe here.

When Isabell got back into the house, she closed the door behind her and for some strange reason she placed the door chain on. Why did she do that? What was the point? Erik would be back soon to take her to the doctor once he dropped Courtney off.

She sighed deeply.

Isabell felt her pulse climb. She turned around and rested her back against the door.

"It's all right, Isabell. You'll be fine, girl. It's all in your mind."

Then...

She heard a sound from the kitchen and jumped.

Someone was in the kitchen. She slowly hobbled toward the back in the direction of the kitchen. The hardwood floor made a creaking sound with every step she made.

"Who's there?"

Oh, God. Please tell me I'm not hearing things again. Please.

Her pulse raced, her stomach tightened into knots. That was the last thing she needed right now.

She glanced at the smart speakers. The light was on. Then she glanced out through the back window into the garden.

She screamed. She thought she saw a shadow, but there was no one there.

Then...

She saw a man. Was it her neighbor? He was out in his yard; she could see him over the low oak garden fence.

Crap.

What was with this neighborhood?

The phone rang, startling Isabell.

She walked over to the phone in the living room. The place was dark, the overcast skies outside wasn't sending much sunshine in so she turned on the lamp by the fireplace.

The name on the caller id read: Sarah P. Morgan and she let out a sigh of relief. *Aunt Sarah.*

"Hello," she said, sitting down in the rocker chair.

"Hey, Isabell. It's your auntie here. How are you doing, Hun?"

She was glad to have company again. "Hey, Aunt Sarah. I'm good. How are you doing?"

"Well. Considering all that's going on, child."

"What do you mean?"

"Hey child, how come you sound so stuffy?" Aunt Sarah dodged the question. "You got a cold or something? Don't tell me you've been crying. Who hurt you? Do I need to come over there right now?"

Isabell grinned and rolled her eyes. Trust Auntie Sarah to always be overprotective when it came to her family.

"Yeah, I've got a cold. But I'll be fine."

"How's the little one? Can't wait to see my grand niece."

"She's good, thanks. She's looking forward to seeing you, too. She's got Grandma's cheeks." *And Granddad's lovely ears.*

"Aww, well isn't that something. Time does fly, doesn't it?"

"I know. Tell me about it."

"Seriously, I'm so glad you finally settled down and got married."

"Um. Well, Auntie I'm not married to Courtney's father, but I am getting married."

Silence lingered on the phone.

"Really now?" her aunt Sarah said with caution.

"Yes, really now. This is the twenty-first century, Auntie. Stuff like that happens you know."

"Well, at least you've got a child. That's a good thing. You know when you got to be in your thirties and still single with no kids, I was beginning to get worried, child."

"Well, there's nothing to worry about."

"No, seriously. I'm glad you have a child now because if you waited too long who knows what could happen. You don't know how these fifty-year-old celebrities are able to get pregnant. You don't know what kind of help they have. But for us normal folks, we can't take chances like that."

Having a family was everything in the Morgan family. If you were single and with no children, something was wrong with you, or heaven forbid, they all would assume you were gay. Not that there was anything wrong with that—well Isabell didn't think so anyway.

She loved reading her romance novels and would dream of the day her Mr. Right would leap off the pages of the book into the pages of her own life. She finally had that with Erik. He lived up to all her fantasies. Caring, loving, a great lover and a body to die for. Did she mention caring?

"Erik's a darling sweetheart. Can't wait for you to meet him," Isabell continued.

"Where'd you two meet?"

"In New York."

"Oh, dear."

"What?"

"Nothing. It's just that...well, what exactly do you know about this guy from New York?"

"Auntie, I know all I need to know."

"How long have you two been dating? How does he feel about you having a child with another man?"

"Well, I'm not with another man now, so he doesn't mind, okay? Besides, Courtney loves him. He's actually really good with children."

Goosebumps sprang up on her arms thinking of how wonderful he was with Courtney. He was almost too good to be true. "He even took her to the daycare for me this morning. It's her first day."

"That's nice. Well, just be careful. "

"Be careful?"

"Yes, child. Be careful who you trust."

"Yes." Her voice was quiet. "Yes, I'll be careful."

An hour later...

A sick feeling tore through Isabell as she paced nervously by the fireplace hugging herself. This was not like Erik to be late. Where was he?

The daycare was only five minutes away. A short walking distance. If only she wasn't limping, she'd have gone with them.

She picked up the landline phone to call Erik to find out where he was, but immediately placed the receiver back down when she saw Erik's cell phone was sitting on top of the counter charging. She squeezed her eyes shut in disappointment, a helpless feeling washed over her.

Crap.

Unfortunately, it was a habit of his to allow his phone battery to go down to one percent before charging then forget to take it with him when he'd leave the house. He wasn't perfect, nobody was. But that always had annoyed her about him, even more so now.

A prickling feeling told her to call the daycare.

"Wendi, please call the daycare," she called out to the smart speaker. It ignored her request. The light was on but the darn speaker wasn't working again.

She searched inside her handbag frantically looking for the phone number for the daycare. Finally, she found the flyer: *Happy Dragons & Bunnies Daycare of Ocean Bay Cove, 1 Garden Green Boulevard.*

She dialed the number and waited for someone to pick up the phone while tapping her fingers nervously on the countertop. The phone kept ringing and ringing.

No answer?

She hung up.

The whole town was giving her the creeps now. What was happening? Why in God's name had she decided to send her daughter to daycare? But she'd checked the daycare out prior to moving to the province. They seemed very friendly, the kids appeared happy and the daycare workers seemed to love their jobs.

The playrooms were fully decorated with beautiful cartoon characters and had lots of fun toys. Colorful mats covered the floors and there was an apparatus for the kids to play on. They had a massive playground she knew Courtney would enjoy. For a small town it sure was very nice facility. Garden Green Blvd was a long street that actually broke off and carried on across from the park. The daycare was situated on the other side. It was about a five to ten minute walk. Isabell grew frantic and dialed the number again.

The phone rang and rang and rang.

She continued to pace nervously. Maybe she should just slip over to the daycare? Pain shot through her ankle reminding her that there was no way she could hobble over there in that condition. Her doctor's appointment was supposed to be at ten o'clock. Erik said he'd take her. Where was he?

He probably picked something up at the hardware store, Isa. Don't get too paranoid.

Something was wrong. She just felt it. Her intuition nudged her.

Isabell dialed the number again and this time someone picked up on the second ring and relief washed over her.

She heard the loud piercing screams of a child in the background.

Then she heard a cheery young woman's voice. "Happy Dragons and Bunnies' Daycare, can I help you?"

"Hi, my name is Isabell Morgan. My daughter was brought there this morning. It's her first day."

Isabell had already filled out the forms when she'd first moved to town. They should have all the information there.

"I'm sorry. I can't hear you."

"My name is Isabell Morgan. I'm calling about my daughter, Courtney."

"I'm sorry, could you please speak louder? I can't hear you. We just had a little incident with one of kids."

"Is he or she all right?"

She heard commotion in the background. Then another staffer came on the phone.

"Hi, it's my daughter's first day," Isabell said. "I just wanted to find out if she's all right."

"Oh yes, yes she's fine. She's fine, she's settling in okay. Don't worry she's not the one crying. She's fine. Listen Sheena is busy right now. Can she call you back?"

Sheena was the daycare supervisor she'd spoken to a few weeks ago.

Isabell sighed a sound of relief.

"Yes. She can call back, thank you."

At least Courtney was at the daycare safe and sound. She was okay. Yet a sinking feeling in the pit of her stomach left Isabell with a heavy spirit.

What's troubling you, Isabell?

Twenty-minutes later, Isabell glanced at the clock. It was now a quarter to ten.

Isabell sighed deeply as she got ready for her ten o'clock appointment. She hoped Erik would be back soon. She didn't want to be late for her first doctor's appointment at the Ocean Bay Medical Clinic.

Isabell adjusted her right hearing aid. She glanced at the clock again. Erik had said he'd pick up some more supplies at the hardware store to fix the broken steps in the basement. She figured he probably stopped there first.

She blew her nose again and wiped her face. She then got into the shower and turned on the faucet. She took a quick warm shower. When she was done, she dried herself off and went to the closet to pull out a black knitted knee length sweater and a pair of comfortable fitted leggings. She changed her mind, not wanting to be in all black, though it accentuated her curves. She decided to pull out the purple knitted fall sweater that also went to her knees and was more like a sweater dress and wore that with the leggings instead. She hobbled down to the main floor and grabbed her handbag and her fall jacket. She pulled that on and looked out the window, hoping she'd see Erik.

She sighed again, glancing back at her watch.

He'd left his cell phone charging in the kitchen so there was nothing she could do. So she decided to write him a note.

Baby,
I've called a cab and gone to the clinic. Talk to you later.
Love you.
Isabell.

She needed to get something for her stuffiness in addition to getting attention for her ankle that looked as if it was more swollen than before. She wanted to make sure nothing was broken and have them run an X-ray. She really didn't want to be late. Isabell called a local taxicab and to her surprise it was there within minutes. She glanced around to look at the place to ensure everywhere was locked up tight. She didn't really trust that guy a few doors down, staring at them every minute.

She then locked the door and gave it a push to make sure it was really locked. She did this three times, part of her OCD and when she felt good enough, she closed the screen door, and then walked down the steps.

The cabbie was such a sweetheart. He'd gotten out of the car and went to the passenger side and opened the door for her.

"Where to Ma'am?"

"The Ocean Bay Medical Clinic, please."

As they pulled out of her driveway, she couldn't help but glance up and saw that the same neighbor guy was looking out his window. At least she thought he was. She saw a shadow at the window then it vanished. Or was that her overactive imagination? She glanced away, looking out at the scenic street as they drove off

She sighed deeply. *Everything will be all right, Isabell.*

Chapter 14

"Is this your first time here?" the redheaded receptionist at the Ocean Bay Medical Clinic asked cheerfully.

"Um. Yes."

"Can you please fill out this form, Ms. Morgan? The doctor will be with you shortly," the receptionist said.

"Thank you." Isabell glanced around the reception area after taking the clipboard and sheet of paper. There were a few people seated there. It wasn't as packed as the city clinics which was a refreshing change.

She looked out the window and saw the taxi cab driver that dropped her off pull out of the driveway of the clinic. He was a cheerful middle-aged man. So friendly.

Erik should have been there with her. Still, she let it slide. He was probably caught up at the hardware store. He had said he needed more material to fix the lower steps of the basement.

She glanced at her watch again and looked out through the glass doors to the outside, hoping that Erik saw her note and decided to follow her there, after he was done doing whatever he was doing.

She had a sinking feeling again in the pit of her stomach.

Nerves.

It was probably nerves. She had to get her thoughts straight.

Your life is what you make it, Isabell. Your thoughts determine your reality.

She filled out the form and paused at the area on the sheet.

Do you or any member of your family have a history of the following: hypertension, heart disease, kidney disease, heart attack, stroke, shortness of breath...

The list went on and she stopped at the bottom of the form:

...drug or alcohol dependency, depression...mental health...

Isabell froze.

Okay, maybe there was something in her family history she didn't want to get into.

Deep breathe, Isabell. In one, two, three, out one, two, three...

She was having an anxiety attack. She'd suffered with them all her life. Would they label her? Would they look at her funny?

She glanced at the sheet regarding the list of medications she'd taken in the past. She was on anti-depressants until she'd weaned herself off of them. She'd began taking them during the abusive years living with her ex-boyfriend. This was a new change in her life. A new beginning.

She was only there today for her swollen ankle—and maybe something for her stubborn congestion. Should she tell them about her family history—about her own medical history?

Chapter 15

Isabell

The taxi driver dropped Isabell back at home at 47 Garden Green Blvd. She couldn't help but feel a pang of disappointment over Erik not showing up at the clinic. Where was he? He'd better be back inside fixing the lower steps of the basement.

When Isabell closed the cab door shut, she struggled to make her way back up the front steps of the porch.

"You all right, ma'am?" the cab driver called out. He was a different guy from the one who'd dropped her off earlier. "You sure you can manage alone?" He looked concerned.

"Yes, I'm fine thanks. My fiancé's inside," she answered hopefully. She hated for him to think she was all alone. When she got up the step she drew in a deep breath and turned the key in the lock. She dropped her keys down on the counter and called out for Erik. "Erik, are you here?"

She thought she heard the sound of hammering on wood but the sound vanished. He was probably in the basement but the atmosphere rung with an eerie silence. Her throat closed up. The banging she thought she heard from the basement went silent. Her lungs burned, her heart exploded in her chest. Terror gripped her and tightened around her neck. Why didn't he answer her back? Was it all her imagination?

Just then she heard a ping sound for text notification and fished into her handbag for her cell phone. Her heart leaped in her chest. Was it Erik?

Her eyes widened with shock as she read the message on the display from then strange zero number 000-000-0000

Then the letter A appeared on the screen followed by another text:

I've got your kid and your fiancé.

I want my brown envelope marked September 25th
Don't do anything stupid.
You'll hear from me soon with more instructions.

Isabell's body went cold.

Chapter 16

Luc

Detective Luc Renald knocked on the door at number forty-seven. The guys from his division had already investigated the text message sent to her phone, which was untraceable. They already looked into the brown envelope the alleged kidnappers wanted, but he was going to probe further. The woman, Ms. Isabell Morgan, insisted on holding on to it and not opening it until the date. Her father had given it to her. He was already briefed on this case.

He glanced around and saw the plants were neatly potted in the front garden. The home looked well taken care of. No sign of abandonment there.

An older woman opened the door. Was it a relative? It was good that Ms. Morgan had someone close by to help her during this time. He only hoped that this story would have a happy ending. It was always rough when a missing person's case happened to involve a minor. A five-year-old at that. These abduction cases were sensitive. He knew all too well.

The AMBER Alert was in full force. Hopefully, they would find her daughter safe and sound. Ms. Morgan also seemed concerned for her fiancé too. Hopefully, there would be some good explanation and they would both be found safe and sound.

"Detective Luc Renald from 57 Division." He introduced himself and showed his badge.

"Oh, please come in, detective. I'm Mrs. Donigan, the neighbor. I just live next door at number 45. It's such a shame about the little girl. She looked so adorable this morning, getting ready to go to the daycare in her pretty pink jumpsuit and her matching Disney Princess coat. What a lovely child."

"She had on a pink jumpsuit and pink coat, you say?" Luc took note of those details.

"Yes, she did. Right this way. I just got here. I'm going to make Isabell some tea."

"Okay, ma'am."

* * *

"This is a recent photo," Isabell said, her lips trembling as she handed Luc a photo of her daughter, moments later.

He nodded with empathy. A sound erupted from the kitchen area and he saw the jolly Mrs. Donigan dancing around while humming and drying the dishes.

There was something very pleasant, yet strange about the neighbor. She was there to console Isabell, yet she seemed to be in a happy mood and doing chores. This was a strange neighborhood.

Mrs. Donigan then wiped her apron and walked into the living area.

"Would you like me to make you some tea, dear?" Mrs. Donigan asked Isabell.

"Um...thank you, Mrs. D." Her voice was faint, weak. As if all the energy had been drained from her body. He wondered if she'd ever be the same again—even if they found her daughter.

"Would you like some tea, detective?"

"No, thank you."

"Oh, no. I insist. You look like you could use a cup. It's the least I could do for our friendly neighborhood officer of the law."

"Okay, thank you." He didn't usually take drinks from members of the community but he didn't have time to stop at Starbucks.

The detective gave Mrs. Donigan an appreciative glance. "Nice neighbors you have here," he said to Isabell, before turning his attention back to her.

"Yes, she is."

"You have any other photos of your daughter?" the detective said. "On your phone?"

"Nothing recent. This is...I don't have my other phone. It was stolen. I didn't have stuff stored on the cloud."

"No worries." Not that he blamed her; he was always cautious what type of stuff he stored on cloud services.

Luc glanced at the photo of the girl. She was adorable. Her tiny curls framed her face. She had rosy red cheeks and large brown eyes framed by long lashes. "She looks just like you," he said.

"Thank you." Her voice was faint; she looked dazed as she peered off into the distance. Was she all there? Of course she'd been traumatized. He tried to get her to be as calm as she could so she could remember as much as possible to help in the investigation to find her daughter and her fiancé.

Luc glanced again at the photograph. There was something very odd that struck him about the girl's jacket. "Nice coat."

"Yes."

"Where did you buy the coat?"

Isabell looked stunned as she peered up at him as if to say how the hell could you ask me this at a time like that? But there was a method to his madness.

"You want to know where I bought my daughter's coat?"

"If you don't mind, ma'am."

She looked stunned. "I don't remember, okay. I...I think it was a gift."

"It's okay, ma'am."

Mrs. D came back into the living room with a tray and two coffee mugs. The tea smelled very inviting, but he didn't think Isabell was in the mood to drink any.

"Here you go, darling," the woman said warmly, motherly. Isabell was lucky to have a caring neighbor such as Mrs. D.

"Thank you," Isabell took the tea absentmindedly. The coffee mug must have been hot, but Isabell held it as if she held a glass of ice water then set the cup down beside her without taking a sip.

"And this is for you, detective," Mrs. D said to Luc.

"Thank you, Ma'am."

The woman gave him a chastising look, probably for having put Isabell through so much in asking his questions.

Luc decided to change his line of questioning for now. If there was one thing he knew, it was that if a person wasn't ready to answer a question, they weren't going to be helpful.

"Can you please tell me what she was wearing this morning?"

"A blue jumpsuit and blue coat."

Luc was stumped. "Did you say blue, ma'am?"

"Yes," she said, looking puzzled. "Why?"

"Because your neighbor there just said she was in pink."

Isabell sighed deeply and picked up her mug. "No. Mrs. D. is lovely, bless her heart, but she doesn't always see too well."

"I see, Ma'am." Luc made a note of that. Something seemed a bit off, but he would get to that later.

Luc took a sip of the tea and immediately spat it out. Isabell did the same thing.

"What the..."

He tried not to swear in front of ladies, but this was a bit much.

"What the devil did you put in this thing, Mrs. D?" he had to ask. That was why officers didn't take offered drinks on the job, but this time was different. He'd just worked a double shift since they were short staffed and he didn't have time to go to the Starbucks off the highway. Their office handled the small towns who didn't have funding for their own police force.

"Oh, um...I thought you wanted sugar."

"Oh, no." Isabell said, slapping her palm to her forehead. "I...I was somewhere else. I didn't even realize you didn't have your glasses on Mrs. D. You probably saw the clear canister and poured salt instead of sugar."

"Tastes as if you poured all the salt from the sea in here," Luc said, reaching in his jacket for his little bottle of water. He often took it along in case he needed to pop a pill for his ulcer.

"Oh, dear. I am terribly sorry," Mrs. D. said.

"No worries, ma'am. Just be careful next time."

Oh, great. He might as well scratch her testimony of the girl in the pink coat. Surely, it was a blue coat as her mother had said. After all, it was Ms. Morgan who'd dressed her own daughter this morning. She should know what her own child was wearing.

"Now, Isabell could you please tell me what your fiancé was wearing. His name's Erik you say?"

"Yes, Erik Joneson. He was wearing a black leather jacket, dark jeans and leather shoes. He..." she sighed deeply. "He has a tattoo."

"Where's the tattoo?"

"On his right arm."

Luc scribbled everything down on his note pad. "Anything else, ma'am?"

"Yes. He's very handsome." He noted her doting eyes when she spoke of her fiancé. "He has a groomed stubble. Beautiful large eyes. High cheekbones. And he has the deepest voice..." She trailed off. She placed her palms on her face.

"It's all right, Ms. Morgan. Take your time."

"It's okay," she sniffled. "I'll be fine. I just want my baby back and my fiancé. I know something's happened to them."

"Right, ma'am." Luc scribbled down some more information.

"Do you have any recent photos of him, ma'am?"

"He didn't like to take photos."

Huh?

"He didn't, ma'am?"

"No. There's this one picture we took though."

She showed him on her cell phone. It was a picture of her in a black vest and he was hugging her from behind. The guy looked very handsome indeed and well-built.

Sorrow clouded her misty eyes.

"It's okay, ma'am we'll try to find your daughter and your fiancé."

"Thank you," she said, her voice weak.

Luc didn't like this one bit. No matter how nice the guy seemed. Something was very off about a guy that didn't like to take pictures, and made sure that everything was in his girlfriend's name. Then this whole bit about being the best daddy to her daughter when he wasn't the biological father. Call him skeptical, but if something seemed too good to be true, it often was in his books.

He'd heard about this stuff when he worked in Boston. Women couldn't be too careful with their kids. There were all kinds of crazies out there. He'd even worked on a case where this guy befriended this woman only to get close to her daughter. The creep even installed cameras in the bathroom right where the shower stall was. He wasn't saying this Erik guy was anything like that. In fact, something told him, it probably wasn't the case at all but still, one had to be very cautious in this day and age.

"We've put the AMBER Alert out to all the media, ma'am."

She looked uneasy.

"Ma'am, is there anything else you'd like to add? Did you two have an argument this morning?" he asked as gently and as tactfully as he could.

She looked offended. "What? No. You think he ran off with my daughter? Erik's not like that. He's very kind. He's all heart. He's a saint."

He resisted the urge to roll his eyes. Men? Saints? Men were good, but he wouldn't call them saints, not even himself. He had been devoted to his ex-wife when they were together. In fact, she was the one that had cheated on him when they'd been together—with his partner.

That was one of the reasons he'd left that precinct and moved to the smaller rural towns to police. He couldn't wait to leave the big city crime anyway, not that the smaller towns were always quiet, like now. When it rained, it poured.

"I'm sure he was, ma'am. But I'm just wondering if you noticed anything strange about him this morning."

"No." She then paused for a moment.

"Actually, he was a bit forgetful. I had to give him Courtney's lunch box for the daycare."

"Lunch box, ma'am?"

"Today was her...this would be her first day at the daycare and she has a special diet. They told me they'd accommodate," she paused to blow her nose. "But I told them I'd pack her favorite foods for the first day." Tears fell from her eyes, spilling over from her cheeks. She was visibly shaken. Her body trembled.

He knew what she was going through. He'd fallen apart, lost his mind when his daughter Jessica had gone missing too. He could also tell that she loved her little girl, as she hugged the stuffed animal to her chest.

He glanced around the home again, there were stuffed toys everywhere. The little girl certainly wasn't lacking for any amusement. Disney DVDs and cartoon movies were scattered about above the unopened boxes. Looked as if they'd made sure the girl's stuff was unpacked first when they moved there.

His heart sank.

That almost never happened. He'd always distanced himself from these cases. But this one was different. He could tell when people were faking emotions, but this woman was dying inside. She was dying slowly before his eyes. She wanted her daughter back safely now. She wanted her fiancé home. She really believed the guy didn't abduct her girl. She really believed somebody might have harmed them both.

He wished he could make it all better for her. She seemed like a nice enough woman. He really hoped this case would end happily. God, he hoped so.

"Do you know anyone who could have wanted to see your loved ones hurt?"

She told him about her ex and the physical and emotional abuse she endured. He'd served his time, but he'd been bitter about it and had promised to ruin her.

She told him her ex saw her as someone he could control and not deserving to be with anyone else. This guy sounded like a complete mess.

After she'd pressed charges he'd apparently told her he'd ruin her one day—if it was the last thing he ever did. He knew how to work the system and pleaded guilty so that he could do less time.

Luc took careful note of every bit of information. They would look into this Jeff character. He had to look at this case from every possible angle.

Unfortunately, the text message to her cell phone was untraceable, but they would keep a close eye on things.

"You need to let us know if you get another text message, ma'am."

"I will." She swallowed hard.

"Now about this brown envelope, ma'am. I noticed the date is marked not to be opened until September 25 of this year."

"Yes, that's right."

"When was this given to you?"

"A couple years ago. Before my dad died. Before both my parents died," she corrected."

"Did he tell you what was in it or why you were not to open it until this year on that date?"

"No. He didn't." She swallowed hard again and shook her head slowly.

Isabell

A wave of in nausea washed over Isabell. Her emotions were out of control again. She thought about her ex and realized there was no restraining order where her daughter and her fiancé were concerned.

Her mind reeled with confusion. What did this mean? Could Jeff have had anything to do with this? Her daughter and her fiancé had to be okay. She didn't know how this evening would end but it couldn't end horribly. It just couldn't.

She thought of Courtney. She's so soft-spoken and so sweet. So friendly. Who could want to harm her?

Guilt weighed her down. The whole situation was a stab at her heart. She shouldn't have let Courtney out of her sight ever. Maybe it wasn't Erik that had the shady past that caught up with him. Maybe it was Isabell. Maybe her ex had caught up with her. Maybe he was going to make good on his promise to destroy her chance at happiness.

It's quite possible she was on the verge of going insane.

"Ma'am, you said your fiancé Erik goes to the Ocean Bay Fitness Center on Main Street?"

"Yes, that's right," Isabell answered dazed, hugging herself. She was going out of her mind, crazy. Her daughter and her fiancé were both missing. Vanished without so much as a trace. As if...

The handsome detective with the disheveled hair and dimples. He reminded her of a young handsome Lieutenant Colombo from that TV series.

Detective Luc slowly shook his head and wiped his brow. Then he scribbled something on his notepad with his pen. He paused for a moment and glanced at his notes as if trying to make sense of her words.

"Ma'am, I don't know how to tell you this but we checked there this afternoon."

"And?"

"They said they saw no sign of him, ma'am."

"What? What do you mean by that?" Her heart squeezed in her chest. She felt the air siphon out of her lungs.

He looked uneasy as if trying to see if he could be as tactful as possible with what he had to say next.

"Ma'am, the desk clerk there said there's no client there who fits the description and it's a pretty small gym. No one there is six-foot five inches, slim muscular build with mousy dark hair and tattoos down his right arm with groomed stubble. No one fits that description. Are you sure that's where he works out?"

Her heart turned over in her chest. Her eyes widened. "Yes, of course he does. Why would he...?"

"Why would he what, Ma'am?" The detective looked expectantly, as confused as she felt.

Why would Erik lie about going to the gym?

Chapter 17

Luc

Mixed emotions seeped through Luc's muscles while he made his way back down the stairs as he pondered what could have happened to the little girl. He'd been upstairs taking a look around. Isabell sat with her aunt now. The neighbor, Mrs. D. had already gone home. He'd be speaking to her again soon.

Luc glanced at the photo on the table. She was a pretty girl. Her tendrils of curls fell over her protruding ears and nicely framed her rounded face. She had the cutest little dimples when she smiled. But there was something about her coat that bothered him in the picture. The little girl should be home safe with her mommy. He was determined to see to that happen.

He gulped. A painful lump climbed into his throat. God help her. God help the person who took her, because that person would need it if he got hold of them.

Stay focused, Luc. Do your job.

It might be a job, but he couldn't help but to take it very personal. His own little girl had been missing. He knew what that felt like - the blame, the shame, the guilt. At least he had his spouse at the time to deal with it together, but who did Isabell have? Besides her estranged auntie and a new neighbor she hardly knew, she had no one. Her other half was also missing. Luc couldn't possibly imagine what she might be going through now.

"Authorities are baffled by the latest incident in Cove County of a man and a child vanishing into thin air," he heard the newscast play on the radio.

"Turn that thing off," he said to an officer.

"Sure thing boss."

He didn't want to risk upsetting Isabell anymore than she was. He could just imagine the sensational spin the media would cast on the case. How could a man and a child just vanish into thin air while heading to a daycare five minutes from their home?

Yeah, he too would like to know that answer. But right now speculation wasn't going to help.

Chapter 18

Isabell

Someone knocked on the door again. The brass knocker made a heavy and forceful sound as it hit the oak wooden front door.

It was getting dark now.

Oh, no.

Courtney was afraid of the dark. Isabell hugged herself and curled up into a fetal position on the couch. The TV was turned off. The last thing she would want was to watch the horror unfold before her eyes by listening the to news reports or any speculation. She wasn't working right now and had changed her cell phone number and wasn't on social media so no one from her past could contact her. Right now, she had to shut the world out to tune into herself. Maybe she should try to lose herself in a TV program. But then again, the AMBER Alert would only flash across the screen. No. No, she mustn't.

"Oh, Child." Aunt Sarah dropped her tiny carry on suitcase at the floor, and pulled her black scarf from around her neck and rushed over to Isabell and pulled her into her arms, hugging her tightly.

Isabell could smell the expensive perfume from her auntie. Her mind was on Courtney. Was her daughter hungry? Had the person who took her fed her? If Courtney were home she would already have a full belly and Isabell would be giving her a bath so she could play with her toys before bedtime. That was what she should be doing right now. Not waiting.

Never in her life before had waiting felt so heavy. Like a never ending torture. The waiting and do nothing game was the worse game to play. And Isabell felt as if she wouldn't win this game. There was no way she could do just nothing.

"How are you doing, honey?" Auntie Sarah looked at her with compassion and concern.

"I...I'm as fine as can be Auntie. We're still just...waiting."

"Of course, child. Yes, I spoke to an officer out there when I got out of the cab. Howdy," she said to Luc. Though Aunt Sarah now lived in Maine, she still had her Southern roots in her.

"Ma'am," Luc said back with a nod.

"Auntie, you really should have let me pick you up from the..."

"No, no, child. Don't be crazy now. You have enough on your plate than having to worry about me."

"It would have gotten my mind off from just waiting."

"It's not your fault, honey. No matter what happens. It's not your fault. You sent your child to daycare with your fiancé and..."

"But what if it is my fault, Auntie?" Isabell's chest heaved.

Why was she taking it out on her auntie who'd just dropped everything in her life to come in from Maine.

"Sorry." Isabell's voice trailed off into a whimper.

"Oh, no. Don't be sorry, honey. Vent. It's good to get it all out. You don't want to be like those psychopaths who can't express normal emotions. It's normal to be sad and grieve when someone is missing...or...well, let's think positive, dear. I brought a few Bible scriptures for you to..."

"Auntie. Please! No offense but I don't want to...."

"It's okay, child. It's okay." Aunt Sarah shoved the small Bible back into her handbag then clasped her hands together rocking back and forth on the couch. She was probably used to the Morgan family not sharing the same faith as she did. Her father, Aunt Sarah's, brother never got along on many things in their life growing up and that had been one of them. That and his drinking, gambling and shady activities—oh, and squandering his share of the inheritance from their parents.

A chill came over Isabell. She had a feeling there was more to this horror than she could ever imagine.

Chapter 19

Luc

"We're going to look into that man you described at the park from the other day, ma'am," Luc said to Isabell. "You also mentioned there were some grown kids at the park bullying your daughter?" Luc continued his questioning, trying to piece together the puzzle of the missing man and child.

"Yes," she said, quietly. "Well, Courtney and I were at the park together—alone. Erik had some errands to do so he couldn't join us."

"I see. Go on."

"There were some other kids in the park. I tried to encourage Courtney to play with the others, but she was a bit shy. She's also a bit self-conscious with her...her beautiful ears," she said, trailing off.

"And?" he asked gently, realizing how difficult this was for her.

She swallowed hard. "There were some young adults. I don't know their ages but...well, they weren't very friendly."

"How so?"

"I don't want you to judge me, detective, and I realize five is way too old for this, but...Courtney always found her soother to be...well, comforting. I tried to pry her away from using it but she would just scream and not speak to me...she has a problem and I need to deal with it carefully."

"I see. No, I'm not here to judge you, Ms. Morgan."

"Thanks," she said weakly. "Anyway, they started yelling and pointing."

"What were they saying, ma'am?"

"Things like..." She sighed deeply and turned her head away. "Big baby and Dumbo."

Big Baby?

Dumbo?

Where's the small town hospitality around here?

Luc closed his eyes painfully, knowing what it was like to be bullied as a kid. From the picture she painted he could see how it prompted the bullying but no child deserved to be treated so cruelly.

"Sorry to hear that, ma'am. It must have been very difficult for you. Did you get a look at the youth?"

"Yes. They wore blue jeans, white T-shirts and jackets from what I saw. I tried not to stare too closely."

"Have you seen any of them around here?"

"I think one of them might live on the street or around here. Not sure."

"I'll look into that. Not sure if they might have seen anything, but we're not leaving any stone unturned here."

"I just want my baby back, detective. I'm going crazy out of my mind. I want my little girl and fiancé back. Where are they? Who took them?" Tears welled in her eyes again, her body trembled as she was consoled by her auntie.

"There, there, child. It's going to be all right. They'll be back soon." Her auntie tried to reassure her.

But was that a promise she could even keep? The more time ticked way, the more it seemed like anything was possible or impossible...

"I hope you find out what happened to them, detective. I want them back home."

"We'll do our best, ma'am. That much I can promise you."

"I never liked the way the people at the park were looking at us," Isabell said.

"Sorry, ma'am? Looking?"

"Yes, as soon as I got into the park, they were just glaring at us. Made us feel uncomfortable. I knew I shouldn't have stayed there."

"Are you sure they were looking at you and your daughter, Ma'am?"

"Yes," she said, her lips trembling.

"Darling, you sure it's not just your paranoia acting up again," her aunt said, probably trying to be helpful.

"I'm not paranoid, Auntie. Not anymore."

"Shh, it's all right, baby," she said, stroking her niece's hair. "It's all right."

"You were close to your grand-niece, Ms. Morgan?"

"Haven't had a chance to meet Courtney yet. But would have loved to."

Would have loved to? Or would like to?

Luc took note of her tense of verb.

"We still don't know if she's...what's happened yet." he offered.

"Of course, what am I saying? I had a daughter, but she died in an accident. Anyway, never got a chance to have grandkids and much too old now so little Courtney would be like my own granddaughter."

"I see."

Isabell got up and paced nervously, staring out the window then hugging herself. Frantic, biting her lower lip, rubbing her arms like a woman going insane. Of course, she would be. Her daughter and fiancé were missing.

He had a hunch Aunt Sarah knew a little more than she was saying...

Chapter 20

Luc

Luc walked around the living room searching for clues. He always observed the type of home a missing child came from. He'd seen all sorts of cases. Sometimes the children were neglected and not properly cared for. They were the ones that were at risk. Their parents sometimes allowed them to carelessly roam the streets. Sometimes the tell tale signs were there.

Sometimes it was somebody they knew that abducted the child. Sometimes he saw evidence of drug and alcohol abuse. But in this case he didn't see any evidence of that. In fact, it was quite the opposite. That was what made this case so strange. The girl obviously came from a good home with a very loving and supportive mother. He was willing to bet that in those unpacked boxes there were tons of happy family photos. The place was very clean considering there were still in the process of moving in.

There were tons of toys scattered all about. It was an open concept living room. There was a massive flat screen TV that had been plugged in. He saw a large overstuffed teddy bear sitting on the couch. Over by the fireplace there was a tiny little toddler table with little toy plates as if the child played with her imaginary friends. The table had place settings of two plates on either side. There was a doll seated on one side and the chair across from it was empty, waiting for the little girl to sit and start a tea party. He felt pain through his heart thinking about his own daughter.

He had to try to get his mind away from thinking of what happened to his daughter, Jessica. His supervisor had asked him again if he wanted to take on the case and he was adamant he could do it. He had to do this. It was part of his job. He didn't want to be handled with kitty gloves. He wasn't emotionally fragile. He was strong. It was as if it gave him another burning desire to make sure he found every single child safe and sound. To heal the hollow feeling inside of him. But he had to shift his focus back to the present. He was there to find a child.

A voice swept into his mind. *Why should he be well-equipped to take this case when he couldn't even find his own child?* He had to dismiss that negative voice. He knew deep down he was well equipped. He could do this. It was very easy to judge parents. He knew that all too well. He's been there before. When his daughter had disappeared everybody immediately blamed the parents for going on outing and leaving the child with a neighbor. That guilt never left him. Of course, it was easy to judge a parent when a child was missing, but he knew all too well that there were some things that was out of their control once a child went out into the world. You could only hope and trust that everything would go the way it should be. If they go to school they should be able to come back home safely. When they go to bed, you shouldn't have to worry about them being kidnapped in the night.

But that was not the case all the time.

He looked around and saw a few cups on the counter, a bag of Princess cookies. He also saw a pink Sippy cup over by the table along with a box of cereal and a kiddy bowl. It looked as if the only things that were unpacked were the child's things. She obviously loved her child very much, especially judging by the toys which he could tell were expensive.

His eyes glanced at the smart speaker on the countertop. He noticed the light was on. He took note of that.

"You said Erik knew about the brown envelope your father left you? Did he tell anyone?"

"I don't think so." Isabell said.

"Did Erik have any enemies?" It was apparent he could have something to do with the abduction, one way or another. Maybe the perps were after him. "It's very rare that a child and an adult would be abducted together."

"That's true, child," her aunt interjected. "Erik was a man walking with his daughter. Who in the world would think about going up to him to steal a kid?"

As much as she didn't want to admit it both her aunt and the detective had valid points. Who would knowingly kidnap an adult and a child? It would be most likely that the adult was the intended target and the child was at the wrong place at the wrong time.

There were so many different scenarios.

"Ma'am, are you all right? Can I get you something warm to drink?"

He knew even offering her hot drink wouldn't do anything to still the chill within her body. He felt that way when his daughter went missing. It was always cold and no one could possibly bring any warmth back into his heart. His heart turned to stone after that. He never looked at people the same way again.

"I'm fine. I'll be fine, thank you." Her voice quivered. "I just want my little girl back."

She'd just told Luc about her sprained ankle and her cold and how her fiancé insisted on taking her daughter to the daycare while she prepared to go to the doctor.

"It was so foggy this morning," Isabell said.

"I know, ma'am. That might complicate things a bit. But hopefully somebody saw something."

She wrung her hands together in her lap looking frantic. Rocking back and forth.

"As I said before, ma'am, we've put out notice at the borders just in case. Unfortunately, time may not be on our side as she could have very well gone missing since she left for the daycare at 9 o'clock, right?"

"Yes, that's right," she sighed deeply.

He could see the weariness on her pretty face. She was a very beautiful woman, very delicate features.

"Honey, why don't you tell him about your condition." Her aunt's voice was filled with anxiety.

"What is that, ma'am?" Luc asked concerned.

"I have a condition called agoraphobia. Sometimes it's not easy to go out to places with crowds or lots of people around."

"She also suffers from a little bit of anxiety, depression and post-traumatic stress dis—"

"This is not about me, Auntie!"

"Sorry, child. I'm just trying to help. I think you need to tell this man everything so he can fully help you, honey."

"We're going to do everything in our power to get your daughter back safely, ma'am, and your fiancé.

He only hoped that it wasn't what he suspected could be. He'd seen so many different cases where the men befriended a single parent just to get to the child. He hoped and prayed Erik was as nice as Isabell believed he was.

Chapter 21

Isabell

"So you called the daycare and they told you she was safe?" Detective Luc arched his brow.

"I'd called them and it was busy there. The woman who answered the phone told me Sheena, the daycare supervisor was busy. They had two sick calls. And couldn't get a replacement. I think there might have been an incident there. There was a kid screaming in the background."

"A kid was screaming?"

"I think he might have fallen. She explained that someone just fell. I heard someone saying, it's okay Tommy."

"And?"

"Well, I told her...I tried to tell her over the noise that my daughter was there for the first time and I wanted to make sure she was all right on her first day. I don't know if she heard me properly."

"Why do you say that, ma'am?"

"Because she kept saying excuse me, I'm sorry, I'm having trouble hearing you...then she just said, yes, she's fine. I don't know if she was just pacifying me. I wanted to go down there, but my ankle hurt. I just decided to trust that she was okay. I would assume they'd call me if she wasn't."

"Only, she wasn't there, Ma'am. Is that correct?"

"Yes."

When he finished up his notes he told her, "We have someone at the daycare now. Sheena, the supervisor?"

"Yes."

"She's devastated. She remembers speaking to you about the openings at the daycare. She told me she was expecting two new kids today."

"*Two* new kids? Oh, no. They probably thought I was the parent of the other child."

"Looks that way, ma'am."

"That's why the worker said, my little girl was fine when I told her," Isabell said.

"It's possible. In any event, Sheena had meant to call you to ask you if your daughter was still coming, but they had two sick calls and things got out of hand."

"I see." Her voice fell.

"Ma'am, we'll do everything humanly possible to bring your daughter back home."

"And Erik. Something must have happened to him. It's not like him."

"Yes, ma'am. And Erik. We're working on finding them both." He then looked at her before leaving.

Chapter 22

Isabell

Isabell's trembling fingers calmed as she held onto the mug of coffee. She couldn't drink, she couldn't even think. The hot drink was only a distraction for her hands to keep them from shaking, because she didn't know what else to do with herself.

She peered out the window. A few cruisers were parked outside. Good thing it was a small town so there was no media circus. A few reporters had stopped by, but the police had dealt with them for her.

She could see some officers across the street going door to door, knocking on the doors of the quiet neighbors asking them questions. Officers with sniffer dogs also roamed the street combing the area for clues. Anything.

This was a nightmare.

Calm down, Isabell. Everything will be all right. There's got to be some explanation. Something.

How could this happen to her? To her baby?

Her gut twisted in agonizing pain. Her poor baby. Guilt ripped the shreds of her confidence. She should've been there for her baby. She should have never left her out of her sight not even for a split second.

Someone must know something. Someone must have seen something. Two individuals could not have vanished into thin air. Or the thick fog. That was the trouble wasn't it? The overcast skies and the fog from this morning only complicated matters, didn't it?

She was going crazy. She was losing her mind. The text message played over and over in her mind like an obsession.

Yesterday, she was just a quiet ordinary neighbor. Hardly anyone on the street knew her tiny family, her fiancé and her daughter. No one even cared to knock on their door to say hello or introduce themselves, except Mrs. D. and Dillon. The others only gaped through their drapes. Wondering who the young city family was that moved into their quiet dwelling, disrupting their peace. Erik loved to blast his music loud in the evenings to wind down. Was that it? Were they disrupting their little peace?

She tried to calm herself by taking some deep Yoga breaths she'd learned in her Yoga introductory course at the gym in the city.

She had to control her thoughts, her therapist once told her.

Were the neighbors in on this? Were they all protecting each other from what they'd done? She'd read way too many horror novels about creepy small towns with citizens who stuck by each other and schemed together to keep outsiders out.

That didn't make sense, but right now, nothing at all made sense to Isabell. It was as if someone knew about her medical past and they were tormenting her, trying to get to her mind - the one thing she fought hard to protect, to keep. Her mother had lost her mind once. It wasn't a happy story. Her father had her committed once. He'd driven her crazy with all the women he'd cheated with. She never forgave him after that. He'd taken control of her finances and used everything for his shady online business. That caused a rift between them, but that was until their deaths. She'd even threatened to leave him at that stage, but he would have none of that.

Isabell dropped the mug on the floor and it shattered into a thousand pieces. She squeezed her head with her hands at her temples.

The noise in her head was too much to bear.

She needed an escape. She was going to lose it, to scream.

How on earth could the detective expect her to just wait and be calm? She wanted her little girl now. She needed Erik now.

Her auntie Sarah came rushing down the steps, her clogs making a clunking sound on the steps of the wooden stairwell, she slipped and stumbled down the last few steps.

"Auntie, are you all right?" she called out, weakly.

"I'm okay," she said, trying to force a cheerful tone. "Are *you* all right? What happened, child?"

"I...the coffee mug slipped."

"Oh, dear." Aunt Sarah ran into the kitchen and grabbed a tea towel and the dustpan and broom.

"It's okay, auntie. I'll do it."

"Nonsense, child. You just go over there and sit yourself down."

Aunt Sarah quickly swept the broken pieces up into the dustpan. "Sit yourself down there, child. Make sure you have your slippers on. I don't want you getting yourself cut on any of the broken pieces. I don't know if I can get them all."

Isabell closed her eyes. Right now she didn't care if she got cut, .it wouldn't feel any more painful than the deep wound in her soul right now.

Isabell never thought it was possible to be alive and feel so...dead. She was dead inside.

Dazed, she sat down on the sofa. Just then her cell phone pinged. Her heart leaped in her chest with excitement.

She reached over to grab it, her heart raced in her chest.

Could it be Erik? A glimmer of hope shone in her eyes for just one moment. Until...

She saw the text message:

B.

It was the letter B. What the hell was that about? She glanced at the screen in shock.

The caller's number was unknown. Probably not even traceable. Another ping sounded and another text message appeared on the screen as she sat in disbelief, her heart racing a mile a minute. Her aunt was busy in the kitchen emptying the remainder of broken glasses into the bin.

If you want to see your daughter
and your fiancé again,

send the cops away.
Keep calm. Keep your mouth shut.
Wait for instructions...

Chapter 23

Isabell

Isabell's eyes widened with fear. Her heart smashed inside her rib cage. Her pulse pounded in her throat.

Send the cops away?

What should she do? Would they hurt Courtney and Erik if she didn't comply?

She knew she had to still involve the cops. It was the right thing to do. It was the smart thing to do. Still, she had to keep silent about the text message for now. The kidnappers were watching her. She had to play it safe.

As each second ticked away, so did Isabell's composure. She was falling apart with every second that passed.

Isabell glanced around nervously. Was she being watched now?

"You must be going through hell, child. Hold strong now," Aunt Sarah said in her Southern accent. Though she lived in Maine, she was a southern girl at heart, born and raised in Texas.

"I don't know who to trust sometimes. I...you're right. Sometimes I think I'd be better off not trusting anyone. It could've been anyone. I don't even trust the authorities."

Isabell eyed the speakers with the light on and tried to remain calm.

Aunt Sarah frowned. "I know you feel helpless, child. But you have to trust them. You have to trust someone."

"But didn't you just say I need to be careful about who I trust?" She arched her brow.

"Yes, but don't take this the wrong way, but honey, have you been taking your medication?"

"I stopped taking them. I don't need them anymore."

"I don't know about that, child. Now you know your auntie loves you very much. Even though I had to keep away from your dad the last few years, but child, it's not possible to live in this world without some semblance of trust. We all need to trust someone or something or we wouldn't be able to function in this world. The trouble is you've got to know who to trust. That's why I told you to come to church with me."

"Oh, boy," Isabell rolled her eyes. "Please auntie. No more talk of church."

"Child, now you listen to me. That's why I pray. The Lord is my Sheppard. We are like sheep out there, child. Innocent sheep going on about our business. We don't know who's a wolf and who isn't while we graze on the grass. We have to ask him to guide us and protect us. There is a spiritual realm out there, child. I know your daddy never believed me, but it's all about doing what's right, because karma is out there. Stuff catches up to people. You don't get away with stuff."

Her father always told her Aunt Sarah was crazy. But she wondered if she had some shred of truth there. The trouble was knowing whom to trust.

"Your daddy put his trust in the wrong folks. Now look what happened to him? Dead as a doornail."

"Auntie."

"Sorry, child. It's just that...well, you need to trust, but verify as one late world leader once said."

"Trust, but verify?"

"Yes, child. But this was way before your time. Anyway, trust, but verify every thing. You can trust people, but make sure you vet them too. Don't just take them at their word. Words can be spoken at a drop of a hat. But what's behind those words? And what about your guy Erik? He might be a nice guy, but what about the people around him? You said he had some kind of a tattoo?"

"Yes." Isabell felt her breath halt.

"Where did he get that tattoo from? Prison?"

"Auntie!"

"What child? I hope you did ask him that question?"

"I didn't ask him that question. He had a stable job back west and moved to make it on Broadway."

"Actor, huh? Well there's your first clue, Sherlock."

"Auntie, that's not fair. Erik is one of the most stable people I know."

"Stable? What exactly do you mean by stable? Stable is relative, you know."

"We can't know everything about everyone."

"But we should. Look at your daddy? Squandered our parents' estate. Foolish man—God rest his soul," she said all in one breath.

Aunt Sarah had always been bitter about that.

Isabell tried not to let the terror strangle her again as she surreptitiously glanced at the text message then at the speakers. Was the kidnapper listening to her now?

Chapter 24

Isabell

"Isabell, please talk to me." Aunt Sarah eyed her with eagerness, trying to get through to her. "Was Erik seeing someone else? What else do you know about this man?"

"Auntie, I've told you once before, he's a really nice guy." Isabell glanced around the house for bugs. She looked out the window surreptitiously. Cops were all around. Lights were on at the neighbors. She would see shadows of people at the windows, staring out from behind curtains or blinds.

"I know, I know. You keep telling me he's a nice guy and I'm sure he is, honey. But people aren't always who they say they are."

Goosebumps spread over Isabell's arms.

"I know, Auntie, but he's different to. Trust me on this one." Silence befell her.

"Honey, I want to believe he's a nice guy. But...okay, let's say he's Mr. Nice Guy. Did he ever tell you he was in any kind of trouble back home? I mean, what twenty-nine year old isn't working?"

"Auntie that's judgmental, isn't it? He's between jobs right now. Besides, he can't work in this country until..."

"Sorry, child." She hesitated as if for a loss for words. "I'm just worried about little Courtney."

Isabell's heart squeezed inside her chest. Her stomach tightened into knots. "I know, Auntie. I'm worried about both of them." Her voice was a whisper, almost inaudible. "Trust me. He really *is* a nice guy. There must be some explanation why he wasn't going to the gym like he said. I really think something happened to both of them on their way to the daycare."

"I know, darling. Listen, please don't mind me. Your dear auntie's just worried about you. It's just that it seems a bit strange that... I mean a grown man and a five-year-old. Five minutes from the daycare and they just go missing? Honey, none of this is making any sense. Either he ran off with her or..."

"I don't think he would do anything to hurt Courtney. He loves her like his own child."

Isabell got up again, hugging herself. She walked over to the window. She remembered when Courtney said she saw a man outside the window. Did she really see a man that night?

Now Isabell may never know.

"Honey, I won't be able to sleep or rest until your little girl is brought home safely." Her aunt was getting as worried as she was.

"I know, Auntie. You and me both."

"I just hope it's nothing to do with one of your dad's business partners."

Isabell spun round, her eyes widened in shock. Her heart skipped a beat.

"What you mean?" Alarm rose in Isabell's voice.

Isabell glanced at the brown envelope with the date marked "Do Not Open Until September 25th."

"This is the envelope I'm not supposed to open until next week."

"Your daddy left that to you, didn't he? An envelope with information about a secret bank account. The key to some stashed money in some foreign account. Yup, that sounds just like my good ol' crooked brother."

Isabell's stomach turned. A wave of nausea swept over her.

No. It couldn't be. Erik was the only other person who knew about the envelope and...

Shit. Shit. Shit.

No.

Her heart felt funny in her chest, beating erratically.

"Honey, I don't mean to get you all worked up or anything, but...I have read books where a victim staged their own kidnapping to get the ransom money and all that..."

"Auntie, please!" Isabell squeezed the sides of her head with her palms, trying to shut out the loud noises in her head. Overwhelming emotions captured her.

"It's okay, child. I'm here for you no matter what." Aunt Sarah hugged Isabell, offering comfort, reassurance. But right now she needed much more. She needed her daughter back. Erik. The truth.

"Let's just deal with one thing at a time. I'm going to go call back that officer in to speak with us. You tell him everything you know and let them handle it, all right, sweetie."

An avalanche of dazed emotions swept Isabell away. She closed her eyes and breathed deeply.

Did Erik stage all of this?

Chapter 25

8:00 p.m.

Isabell

Her auntie was right, what *did* Isabell know about Erik's past?

She could never live with herself if she put her trust in the wrong person to take care of her little innocent baby by not fully knowing his background. Then again how much *could* you really know about someone? Her mother and father were married forty years and there were still some things that her mother never knew about her father.

"You going to be all right, child?" Aunt Sarah tried to stifle a yawn, but it didn't work.

"Yes, I'll be fine. Please go to bed. I'll be fine."

"You sure?"

"Yes." Her voice was quiet.

"Okay, but please let me know if you need anything at all. Anything now, you hear. And I'll get it for you."

"I need my baby back, Auntie."

"Yes, well except that, child. I ain't the police. Aww, child, sorry, I didn't mean to sound so..."

She sighed heavily. "It's all right, Auntie. I'm just emotional right now. I want Courtney back right now. I need Erik back."

It stirred her up inside that she had no clue as to where they were or what they were doing now. It was bedtime. Usually around this time, they'd be reading Courtney her bedtime story. Then they'd tackle unpacking another box before making some tea and evening snacks and curling up by the fireplace in front of the TV watching a Netflix show.

But damn!

This was not how the evening was supposed to turn out. Her family was missing. Gone without a trace. But how?

"I know I can't bring her back this instance, baby, but..."

94

"I know you're only here to help me." Isabell held herself again. Pacing back and forth.

Aunt Sarah walked over to Isabell and wrapped her arms around her shoulders. And Isabell couldn't help but leaning into her. Just like old times. Only these were more troubling times.

"And what if they don't find them? What could've happened?"

She didn't even know if they were in the area or somewhere across the country by now, or across the border, but Courtney didn't have a passport.

"I don't know child. But there has to be a reasonable explanation for all of this. I mean, I watch a lot of soaps and movies, but I ain't never seen anything like this before. A grown man taking his stepchild to the daycare five minutes away then poof! Vanishes into thin air. Oh, child. What has this world come to? Good thing I don't believe in aliens cause..."

"Auntie!"

"Oh, sorry child. Hush now." She patted Isabell's head as she'd done when she was a child and trying to comfort her.

Only the more she patted her head, the more it hurt. It didn't help much now.

She glanced at her cell phone waiting for the letter C since the creep seemed to be making this some sort of alphabet game. She reached over to plug out the smart speakers but the light remained on.

Still no new text messages.

Chapter 26

Isabell

Isabell heard a ping sound on her cell phone, her heart pounded in her chest as she ran to look at it. It was another text message.

Thank God!

She'd begun to think the kidnappers had abandoned her and cut off all communication since she hadn't complied with their first request to send the cops away.

She gazed at the screen in shock. The hairs on her neck stood up. It was the letter C followed by another text message...

> *Hello Isabell*
> *You've been a bad girl.*
> *You didn't send the cops away.*

She texted them back:

I couldn't. I didn't tell them about that text message. Is my baby all right? Is Erik okay?

She received another text:

> *Smart move.*
> *Yes. And Yes.*
> *She's just fine. He's just fine.*

Her heart raced like mad, at least they were okay. Thank heavens for that. She then heard another ping and another text message appeared:

> *I need to have that brown envelope marked with the note "Do Not Open until September 25th".*

No funny business with the cops or you'll never see your daughter and fiancé again.

I'll send a message with more instructions.

Isabell's blood ran cold.

She texted back then deleted it. She should let the detective know first. She wanted to ask the kidnappers if they were nearby, but for some reason terror gripped her. If she pissed him off, he might hurt them. She could not breathe, her lungs burned, her body temperature dropped, her limbs felt numb.

Okay, calm down Isabell. They're safe for now. That's good.

She didn't care for that damn cursed envelope anyway. Whatever was in it meant nothing to her. Why had her father left it to her anyway? She wanted her daughter and her fiancé back. That was all that mattered. Whoever it was could keep the damn envelope and whatever was inside it.

"What is it, child? What's wrong?" Aunt Sarah's voice interrupted Isabell's thoughts as she came back into the kitchen.

Speechless, Isabell showed her auntie the screen.

A ping sounded and another text message appeared on the screen.

D.
You need to be careful who you trust, Isabell.
Make sure your aunt doesn't say anything
or you'll never see
Your daughter again. Or your man.

Aunt Sarah's eyes widened with shock.

Isabell brought her hand to her mouth. Terror gripped her throat. She couldn't breathe or swallow.

Isabell glanced at the smart speakers, then she glanced at her auntie.

She *was* being watched.

She was being *watched* and listened to.

"He can see us or hear us, can't he?" Her aunt Sarah's mouth fell open. Isabell could see the look of terror on her face. It was the same terror Isabell felt.

Who was this monster?

It had to be someone close by.

On the one hand, her daughter and fiancé were alive. Or were they? So, Erik didn't abduct Courtney after all. She knew it all along, didn't she? It was someone else.

"I was right," she whispered. "Something's not right about this town. I could feel it when we first got here. Oh, Auntie."

"Now, now. Calm down, child. It's just your paranoia. It's got to be someone who got hold of your number after the media report."

"But he knows you're here *now*. He can...he can hear us..." she whispered. If she grabbed the speakers and threw them out, that might piss off the kidnappers and she didn't want them to take it out on Courtney and Erik.

"Well, I've heard of neighborhood watch, child. But *this* is creepy."

Isabell wanted to cry.

"It's all right, child. It's all right."

This didn't seem real. This stuff only happened in television dramas or in the movies, but not in real life. Nothing seemed real. Was this a prank? But what if it wasn't? What was she going to do now?

What was this really about?

Just the envelope.

Now she was more curious to find out what her father had given her. Was this about an associate of her father's?

Or had someone from Erik's past been watching him? Did they have him under surveillance?

Did his past, the one she knew nothing about, catch up with Erik? She'd read stories about gangsters starting a new life in a new suburb, a family life, then all of a sudden...they're found dead on their driveway, a string of bullet holes in their body. It happened all the time and the neighbors would say the man was such a nice quiet family guy. But was his past nice and quiet? That was just it. What did Isabell really know about Erik's past?

If he were here right now, she'd kill him for putting Courtney's life in danger like that. If he really was involved in shady dealings in the past he should have been upfront with her from the beginning. She'd asked him about his tattoo, but he never elaborated. He'd told her it was only something he did in his late teens. Really? What teenager got a tattoo like that? What kind of background did he have? How did his parents allow him to have that?

But then he seemed so caring, so kind, so compassionate in every way. This didn't mesh with the possibility that he was shady. He was always kind to the homeless, so helpful around the house and even with their neighbors before they moved to Ocean Bay Cove.

* * *

A few moments later, Isabell searched for her old pill bottle in one of the unpacked boxes from the last time she'd seen her therapist. She never did finish the remaining pills after her parents' tragic deaths. But she'd kept the medication, thank God. Whoever was sending the text messages were coding it so it wasn't traceable. Clearly they were dealing with a professional.

She needed her pills right now.

She once read somewhere that some pills could go way past the expiration date. Not that it had expired. But right now, she needed to calm her nerves. Her anxiety. If she'd known this was going to happen she would have asked for a prescription for anti-anxiety and anti-depressants. But no one could predict the future.

"What you looking for, child?"

"I need my pills."

"No, you don't child. You know how I feel about those mind medicines."

"I think I'm going to have a nervous breakdown, Auntie. I don't even know what to do now. We're being watched. I don't even know if I can trust the detectives now."

"Oh, boy, here we go again, child. You can't *not* trust the detective, Isabell. He's here to help you."

"Really? Then why did I just receive this text message about not trusting anyone? That's exactly what he told me. Not to trust anyone."

"Then why would he give himself away, child?"

Was it possible that she'd been watched even before today?

She stopped looking for the pill container and looked underneath the couch then searched her house and pulled up pillows.

"What are you doing now Isabell? Have you lost your mind?"

"Yes. My mind's completely gone, Auntie. She pulled up the pillows, searched the tables and looked on the ground, running her hands under the couch. "I'm looking for a wire. A bug."

"Oh, dear Lord, please help my niece. I know mental illness runs in the family, but please spare her, Lord."

Isabell ignored her Auntie and continued to search frantically. She then gave up and crouched down on the floor, hugging her knees to her chest. Her auntie knelt down beside her, stroking her hair.

"It's going to be all right, child. It's going to be all right."

Was it?

Why did Isabell have the sinking feeling that this was just the beginning of her nightmare?

Chapter 27

Isabell

Isabell's mind raced, her head pounded. She kept her gaze fixed on the screen of her cell phone hoping for another text message soon with the letter E.

Wait a minute, what was she doing?

To hell with the kidnapper. She'd read that one should never negotiate with them. Cops were pros at handling these situations, right? The crooks would probably only betray her once they got what they wanted. She was going to keep them involved, but not yet, not while she was being watched.

Keep calm, keep your mouth shut?

Her heart hammered in her chest.

An hour after the detective left again, after she'd filled him in on more information about the envelope, she was ready to go upstairs. There was no use in hanging out in the family room.

The family room.

The irony of it all was that her family was the one thing missing. She could picture Erik lounging in the couch with the remote, on his cell phone. Courtney sitting close up to the TV. Even though there were tons of unpacked boxes off to the side, they'd made sure the family room had lived up to its name so far.

With heavy feet, she dragged herself up the stairs.

A chill ran down her spine as she glanced at Courtney's bedroom. She was haunted by her little girl. She needed to see her now. Where was she? Emotions welled in her throat. She thought she couldn't possibly survive this. Who would do this? Who would take her little girl away from her?

Terror gripped her throat and squeezed tight. She couldn't breathe. Her muscles tensed. Her blood ran cold. Nothing would make her better now until she got her daughter back.

She stood outside the doorway to Courtney's bedroom. There were so many boxes still unpacked, but she and Erik made sure that Courtney's things were the first to be unpacked.

She stood at the door, unable to move. She pictured her daughter sitting on the bed playing with her stuffed toys. She could hear her daughter's tiny voice as she looked up and said, "Hi Mommy."

She made her way into the room looking around, hoping that she would see Courtney. What she saw was emptiness. What she *felt* was emptiness.

She inched over to Courtney's bed and looked at the beautiful pink covers with the cartoon characters on them. A river of tears spilled over from her eyes. She looked at the pillow where her daughter had laid her head last night. Where was her daughter going to lay your head this night? She wished she knew. She wanted her daughter back home with her now.

Would the police be able to find them in time? If only she'd taken Courtney to the daycare herself this morning. But she had to go down to the basement and sprain her ankle, didn't she?

Her heart was heavy with guilt. The guilt tore at her spirit. Leaving her with lacerations on her soul.

She sat on the bed, a tsunami of dread washed over her.

She wanted to be alone right now. She knew that her aunt had come to help her out, but she really needed to be by herself. The pain was so great that nothing and no one could calm her. The only thing that would was her daughter and her fiancé safe at home. But would she ever see them again?

She felt hollow inside. This couldn't be happening. This was a dream. She couldn't believe this was her reality now. She felt empty as the house.

Her eyes darted across the room and drank in the surroundings. She saw her daughter's toys scattered around. The bag of pull-ups on the dresser. Her daughter's cute little Disney comb and brush set.

She was a tormented soul right now. She hugged herself while seated on the bed, rocking back and forth.

Her mind drifted back on the text message.

They're gone. They're gone.

Restless, she got up again and wandered around the room like a crazy woman. Her mind had drifted to her daughter's favorite doll. She picked up the doll as if the doll would shed some answers.

She sighed deeply.

Isabell glanced over at the opened closet and saw her daughters clothes neatly lined up. She swallowed hard but the lump would not go down in her throat. She was always an obsessive-compulsive person. She had her daughter's clothes all lined up for the first week of the daycare. Would her daughter ever get a chance to wear those clothes?

Courtney was such a sweet quiet little kid.

She glanced over at the bookshelf. Courtney loved to read her books like her mommy. She liked to escape in the stories. Just as Isabell had done when she was a child. She didn't have many friends just like Courtney.

She heard the door creak open and turned around, the sound interrupted her thoughts.

"Darling, are you okay? What are you doing here alone? You shouldn't be in here." Her aunt's voice carried an echo of concern in her tone.

"I'm fine Auntie. I'll be fine."

"You really need to be with someone right now. I don't want you alone. I worry about you all the time."

"I'll be fine, Auntie. Really."

"How could you say that darling? I know you're being brave but you must be going through a lot of hell right now. I just want you to know that I'm here for you. It's okay to cry, it's okay." Aunt Sarah started to cry now. "It's okay to be scared. But darling, I know that everything will be okay. That little Courtney will be back. She'll be back with us and she'll be safe."

"What if she doesn't come back to us?" Even though Isabell spoke the words she didn't want to believe it. She didn't want to believe that her daughter would never come back to her. How could fate be so cruel to her? After all that she'd been through in her life?

"Oh darling, sometimes we just have to trust."

"Trust? Trust that everything will be okay?"

"Sometimes we just have to darling. Sometimes trust and hope are all we have if you want to survive in this world."

"Unless you trust the wrong people. Or the wrong town."

9:35 p.m.

Luc

Time was running out. Luc continued making his rounds going door to door talking to neighbors on the street. He went back to Mrs. D's house. She'd mentioned she heard Erik banging all hours of the night. The woman seemed very odd.

She'd lived there for over forty years with her husband and their adopted daughter. But there'd been some domestic dispute calls on a few occasion.

Turned out the old man wasn't very well-behaved. He'd been seeing his adult adopted daughter on the side. How long had that been going on? No one knew.

Sadly, the daughter and husband had vanished. There was never a missing report filed, not by Mrs. D anyway. The daughter worked at the local grocery store and when she didn't show up to work one day, they called home. Mrs. D had told them that she left town with her father, Mr. D. Now the strange part about that case was that there was no trace of them anywhere. No sign of anything. There was no evidence they'd packed up their stuff to go, but the authorities had

very little to go on. Apparently, Mr. D. had spoken about leaving town
before. He'd actually told a friend he was going to be leaving with his
own daughter—adopted daughter. After that, no one ever heard from
them again. There was no evidence of foul play and they couldn't get
a search warrant to search the grounds of the house. Sometimes things
just didn't add up.

Luc took out his notepad and began scribbling.

"Can I get your full name again, ma'am?"

"Leanna Donigan. You can call me Mrs. D," she beamed. "Can I get
you some coffee or tea, Detective?"

"I'm good for now, thank you." Had she forgotten about the last
cup she'd made for him?

"It's such a shame about that nice young man and his...his
stepdaughter, isn't it? I do hope they find them safe and sound. What
do you think could've happened to them?"

"We're not yet sure, ma'am. Now you said you saw them leave here
around nine o'clock in the morning?"

"Why yes. The lady, Ms. Morgan. She's such a nice neighbor. Very
quiet. Very kind. Anyway, she saw them off at the door and I...yes, that's
it. I think the man forgot something for the girl so she ran back into
the house and fetched it."

"Can you tell me what that was, ma'am?"

"Yes. It was a pink lunch box. That's what it was, right?"

"Yes, Ma'am."

"Okay." She sipped her coffee and placed the small cup back on
the saucer and sat leaning forward in the chair. Her silver white hair
was silky and piled up on a bun. She seemed rather neat. A typical
grandmother-type. Pleasant cheeks. She reminded him of the cartoon
granny from the old Bugs Bunny show minus the blue dress and
spectacles. He glanced over at the table by the lamp. She had spectacles,
just not on her.

"I notice you have a pair of glasses, ma'am. Is that for reading?"

"Oh, dear. There they are," she said, feeling on the table for it.

He reached over and handed her the pair.

"Thank you so much. Sometimes I have trouble with seeing up close." She chuckled.

Well, there went his eye-witness testimony. Seemed like Mrs. D saw what she wanted to see, whenever she wanted to see it.

"I waved to the little girl and she waved back to me. She was such a lovely little thing. So adorable. Lovely child." Sorrow flashed in her dark grey-green eyes. "Too bad really."

"What's too bad, ma'am?"

"About what happened to them?"

"Do you know anything else, ma'am?"

She thought for a moment.

"Did you see anything suspicious?" he probed. "Or anyone in the neighborhood you haven't seen before." He gave a quick look at her glasses in her hands on her lap. She'd taken them off again.

Well that's just great.

He hoped she would have seen something that could help the case.

"I...I went back inside my house and then...I heard the screeching of brakes on a car."

He scribbled down the notes. "Screeching of brakes?"

"Yes. You hardly hear that around here, you know. Everyone drives very carefully around here. It's a nice quiet neighborhood. I've been here for over forty years, you know. Earnest and I bought the home together. We were so happy here." Her tone turned bitter. "We were alone. Everyone kept looking at us as the childless couple. Anyway, we adopted our little girl." Her expression turned unreadable.

He was going to probe further about the car, but then he wondered why Ms. Morgan hadn't heard it. Then again, he remembered her telling him to speak from her left since her right ear had severe hearing loss. Her ex had done that to her. He didn't take too kindly to any man who'd lay a finger on a lady. Period. He'd gotten into trouble once trying to break up a domestic fight before.

"You also mentioned you heard him hammering late a night?"

"Oh, yes. You can hear through the walls, you know. These joined homes. Anyway, he'd be hammering late at night."

Luc couldn't believe it. What had that man been working on in the basement? Did it have anything to do with his disappearance? He sure as hell wasn't fixing those broken steps in the basement. If he had been, perhaps Isabell wouldn't have stumbled and fell through one of the lower steps and twisted her ankle. Was he setting up some sort of trap. He scratched his forehead. This case baffled him like no other.

The woman yawned. She was obviously getting tired. Probably a sun downer.

"I'm going to follow up on this, Mrs. D. Please let me know if you see or remember anything else." He handed her his card.

"Yes, .will do. I'll be going over next door to check on Isabell later. Ms. Morgan," she clarified.

"That's awfully nice of you, ma'am. Very neighborly."

"Well, that's what good neighbors are for, detective. We stick together."

When Luc got up, his feet stumbled over something. It was an empty pill container. He picked it up and glanced at the prescription then handed it to Mrs. D.

"Are you sure you'll be all right, ma'am?"

"Yes. I'll be fine."

He wondered how a lady with such ailments and forgetfulness could get on without any trouble. Still, she'd been there for almost as long as he'd been alive so she must be doing something right.

"Please let us know if you need anything at all, ma'am."

"Will do, detective. I know the number." She winked.

For some reason, he couldn't tell why, but he felt a slither of discomfort. Something was nudging at him. If only he knew what it was.

9:45 p.m.

The woman at number eighty-five wasn't home earlier so he was glad to see the light on in the house now. She was probably a shift worker.

When she gazed at the picture of Courtney, taking it into her hand, she shook her head and tsked. "Sweet little girl. Saw her around, but not much. Hardly saw them people," she said.

The woman wore blue jeans and a vest and had tattoos down her right arm and up her neck. She also looked to be in her mid-thirties.

"You hardly saw them, ma'am?" the detective asked.

"Yeah," she said, taking a swig of beer from a can. "Hardly saw 'em. They keep to themselves like most people these days. Don't know who to trust nowadays. You hear so many things. It's better to keep to yourself these days..." she rambled on. "You can't get too close to people these days, you know..."

Luc nodded in acknowledgment as he took notes.

"When did you last see them?"

"The guy's kind of cute though. The woman is..." the woman wrinkled her nose. "She's an oddball, ain't she?"

"Excuse me?"

"Whenever she's walking alone, she just...talks to herself a lot. She's just...I don't know...weird."

Weird?

That wasn't the best way one would want to be described by a stranger was it?

He sighed deeply. "Thank you for your time, Ma'am. If you hear anything or see anything out of the usual or remember anything else, please let me know," he said, handing her his card.

She took it and looked thoughtfully. "Will do. Is this going to be on the national news?"

He looked at her, brow raised.

9:55 p.m.

Luc took another swig of his Starbucks coffee. One of the officers grabbed a cup for him a few minutes ago. He made his way over to number eighty-seven on the street, while the other officers combed the area. When he walked up the pathway toward the porch he thought it heard a clucking sound.

He saw a cute blue-headed parrot in a cage through the porch window. He had the most adorable wide black round black eyes he'd ever seen on a parrot. The bird started clucking again, then made a squawking sound, followed by some tongue clicking. The type of sound was similar to what a human clicking his or her tongue on the roof of the mouth would sound like. It meant the parrot was either happy or seeking attention or both. Not all parrots made that sound. He had an uncle who owned a nice African Grey parrot back west.

"Shut up, Rex!" a gruff man's voice sounded.

Rex, the parrot, huh?

"Leave him alone, Charlie. He's just expressing himself."

"Damn bird. Why d'you have to get a freaking parrot?"

"Well, someone needs to be friendly around here."

Luc rolled his eyes and shook his head.

"Hey there little fella," he said warmly to the parrot who was propped on his swing in the cage. The parrot had blue and grey and orange feathers and a sweet little curved grey beak. Luc was an animal lover at heart, birds, animals, you name it. He trusted animals more than humans sometimes. And why not? Humans were the only beings that hunted each other, did terrible things to one another for the most asinine reasons. Not birds, certainly not birds.

The parrot squawked.

"Hey there little fella." Luc grinned, warmth crept inside him for the first time today, despite the seriousness of his visit. It was nice to have some friendliness injected into his already troubling day for a change.

Was this a sign that things could look up? He sure hoped so.

"*Squawk*. Hey there little fella. *Squawk*. Hey there little fella." The parrot's voice was loud and forceful. So this little guy really liked to mimic strangers, huh?

"Shut. Up!" He heard the man's voice shouting from inside again.

The bird was in a cage on the enclosed veranda. Probably to get some air. It was awfully trusting of this couple to leave their bird outside likes this.. Blue-headed parrots were an expensive breed. If this were the city...

Yeah, if this were the city, more people might have seen something or captured it on their smartphone or security camera. It seemed people were always recording something nowadays.

Luc knocked on the door.

He heard footsteps on the hardwood floor making their way over to the door. A woman came to the door. She was wearing a housedress with an apron over it, her hair rolled up in curlers. Luc figured she must be in her mid-sixties.

"Good evening, ma'am," he said, showing his badge and introducing himself.

"Oh, dear. Detective, is everything all right?" She looked panic-stricken. He smelled the scent of burning cigar smoke coming from the back.

"No, ma'am. There is a child missing and an adult."

"Oh, dear, please come in."

"Child missing. *Squawk*. There is a child missing."

Luc wiped his brow and rubbed his forehead.

"Oh, please don't mind Rex. He sometimes repeats things. We just got him a few months ago."

"Who is it?" the man's voice sounded again. The sound of TV in the background played low.

"It's the police. A child is missing."

"What?"

"A child is missing," she called out annoyed. "Turn the damn TV down."

"You turn that damn parrot down first."

Luc thought it was strange that the man only now just turned on the TV or turned it up.

"What's this about a child missing?"

Luc explained as much as he needed to the woman. The man soon appeared. He looked as if he'd just rolled out of bed, his hair disheveled and he looked as if he hadn't shaved in weeks. He wore an old vest with holes in it and pajama pants. A half-burnt cigar hung from the corner of his lips. He had a beer in his right hand.

"What's this about?"

Luc explained again. "Have you seen the child or anything suspicious?" he asked.

"Oh, the child from down the street? The new neighbors?" The woman clutched her chest with her hands. "Oh, no. Not Courtney."

"You've seen her, ma'am?"

"That kid that always left her bike here?"

He nodded. "You've seen her?"

"She always comes to talk to the damn parrot."

"Rex. That's Rex, Charlie. He's not a damn parrot. He has a name, you know."

He resisted the urge to say all right, all right, no need to argue here, but he was not refereeing right now.

He redirected the conversation back on track. "The girl, ma'am. When did you last see her?"

"Courtney would come here a lot in the past week to play with Rex. She really liked him. He'd start singing. Her mother would be looking for her and frantic. She'd have so much fun with the bird that she would forget to take her things home."

"Forget what things, ma'am?"

"I don't know. She left her doll here once. And her bike."

"Her bike, ma'am?"

"Yes. Her mother wasn't very happy about that one evening. She'd apologized so profusely. I told her it was all right. Courtney's such a quiet kid. So quiet and well-behaved."

Luc wandered how such a caring and protective mother like Isabell could allow her five-year old to wander down the street alone even if it's to the neighbor's home. Something didn't add up. Was she taken there? He could imagine her riding her bike, playing around near the front then wandering a couple doors down where she heard the squawking sounds of a parrot.

Curiosity maybe?

"*Squawk*. Courtney look. *Squawk*. Courtney look. *Squawk*. Courtney look."

Chills ran down Luc's spine. There was something eerie in the way the bird said those words.

Courtney look?

Was the bird saying Courtney should look out?

He wished he could have asked the bird what the little girl's state was. Was she alone? Did she looked frightened? Was she lonely? Neglected? But judging by the expensive items of clothes in her closet and her expensive new bike with training wheels, the tidiness of the home, despite the unpacked boxes strewn about, he didn't get that impression.

This would be the most complex case he'd ever worked on. He was sure of it.

10:15 p.m.

Luc didn't have to get too far before seeing a van parked down the street. It was from the local furniture store on Main Street. He shuffled his way down and saw there was a man sitting on the front porch.

"Good evening, sir," Luc said to the man. He then showed his badge. "I'm Detective Luc Renald from 57 Division. I'm here about a missing girl and her stepfather."

The man didn't seem to phased or too surprised. Luc found it very odd indeed.

He hadn't been in that town long, but there certainly was something strange about Ocean Bay Cove. So different from the city. He thought the city was unpredictable, but that was nothing in comparison to this place.

"Yeah," the man said in a cool dry voice.

"You see anything suspicious, sir?" he asked calmly.

The man curled his lips downward and shook his head slowly. "Nope. Haven't seen anything funny. Except the family down the street."

"How so?"

"Nothing. Just a very strange family." He then reached into his pocket and pulled out a box of cigarettes he flipped the top open and took one out. He then took out a gun shaped lighter from his other pocket then pulled the trigger and a flame shot out and lit his cigarette. He then took a deep inhale and blew out a puff of smoke.

Luc didn't really care too much for his attitude. He had a bad feeling about this, but he kept himself professional. He was on police business.

"Can you tell me where you were between the hours of nine and six today, sir?"

"Yeah."

"Where were you, sir?"

He was one of those guys, huh? Luc could always pick up on anti-cop types.

"I was out delivering, as usual. We small folks have to work to make a living."

"I hear you."

"It's sad about number 47 with the little girl missing on her way to the daycare with her daddy."

Luc stood still for a moment eyeing the guy skeptically. He knew a lot. Probably heard from the news.

He then fixed his attention back to Detective Luc. Void of emotion.

"It was her stepfather."

"Oh, my bad. Thought he was her real father."

"No, sir."

He watched the guy's response carefully.

Luc was going to have to keep a very close eye on the delivery guy.

"You work at the local furniture store?"

"Yeah, I work at the store. We're busy around here, especially at this time of the year, when a lot of people are moving with kids going back to school and everything."

"I see."

"There's been a lot of forecloses on the street."

"There has?"

"Yeah. There were some crazy criminal types coming out here buying up some nice houses with dirty money. Up to no good. We have a pretty good neighborhood watch around here."

Good neighborhood watch?

Funny how it missed seeing the girl and her stepfather walking to school in broad daylight this morning.

"It's a shame not one of the houses have a security camera on the street."

"Don't need one in this neighborhood."

"It would have come in very handy today, sir."

"Indeed." His voice was callous. Emotionless.

"What happened to the criminals you saw on the street?"

"Well, I guess you could say they ended up moving. Not paying bills what have you. City took a few of the properties."

That was the trouble with a small town right? One of the benefits was that everybody who everybody was. Everybody knew when there was a newcomer. And everybody knew each other's business. The trouble was that could be a good thing or...a bad thing.

Call him a skeptical, but in his line of business he'd seen the worst of humanity. He'd seen things that would make anybody's head spin and stuff that would keep them up late at night fretting.

It was because of his line of work that he was so untrusting of others. Sometimes the ones who hurt the victims were the closest to them. Not all the time, but enough times to make one wonder.

Right now the only thing that was driving him was the burning desire to see this child return home to her mother's arms, safe and sound. He wanted it more than anything. He obsessed over it. He was going to find that girl alive even if it killed him.

How the hell could a girl and her stepfather, a big strapping 6'4" guy the shape of a quarterback, go missing in this nice cozy quiet town? That was the question of the century.

Nothing was adding up.

Nothing.

Someone was lying to him. But who?

As Luc left, he glanced back and saw the man staring back at him. Then the man looked away and stared into space. He drew on his cigarette and blew out round puffs of smoke.

Luc felt a chill down his spine. He didn't like that man one bit. He didn't trust him.

10:25 p.m.

"Aww, what a shame. That man was such a nice young fella," the woman at the house a few doors down said, clutching her hand to her chest, tilting her head to the side.

"*Was*, ma'am?"

"Well, you know...he was killed right?"

"I didn't say that, ma'am?"

"Oh, well....good. He's a nice guy, by the way," she said, poking her head out the door. "Is this going to be on the news? Am I going to be on the news? Where are the cameras?" She started to fix her blond curls.

Luc resisted the urge to roll his eyes. Given the seriousness of the situation, he wished he could say he was stunned, but he'd seen all types. Especially whenever there was a sensational case that garnered lots of attention.

Some folks always wanted to get in on the action. A lot of people were like that. Sometimes they embellished the truth or added themselves into historical occurrences to add a sense of importance.

Nobody wanted to miss being a part of history. Imagine if this garnered international attention?

They all wanted to be part of it in some way. He just hoped he could get some information that would help in this bizarre missing persons case.

"When was the last time he saw him, ma'am?"

"I think I saw him last week," she said as if trying to remember. "He was walking down the street with his daughter. He was very friendly, you know, always smiling. What a sweet man. What a shame, a pity. And just the other day he even offered to cut my grass."

"He did, ma'am?" Luc was surprised.

"Oh yes. My husband Stan passed away some time ago and it's been difficult since my back injury. Sometimes I have to pay people to come and help me. The grass is getting taller and he offered and I told him that it would be fine. If his wife didn't mind. What a sweet guy he was."

"Ma'am, you keep saying was, we haven't established his whereabouts yet or anything else."

"Yes. Right, of course." She flushed.

Detective Luc didn't let that slip by him, the fact that she referred to a man in past tense.

"I'm sorry I referred to him in past tense. Bad habit. I don't know anything I mean you said he was missing so I assumed well, that's all I know..."

"Yes, ma'am. Thank you for your time. We'll be in touch. Please let us know if you remember anything else."

"Yes. Of course." She looked a little uneasy and embarrassed.

Seemed like she could have been embellishing a lot of information. He didn't think she meant anything by it, but she really needed to not get too over excited. The last thing he would wanted was for somebody to mess up the case—or leak false information to the media. Things happened at lightning speed time these days.

He'd seen it happen before, witnesses giving false testimonies trying to embellish the facts and put themselves in the situation. He even once saw an accident case with bystander intervention. Everybody had their own perception of what happened and overemphasized their own role in helping the victim even if they were never near that person. It happened all the time unfortunately. Human nature.

10:35 p.m.

"Oh yes, the nice lady at number 47. Nice family. Quiet," the neighbor at number ninety-two said to Luc.

"When was the last time you saw her or her daughter or fiancé, sir?"

The man scratched his forehead. There was a dog barking in the other room. "Stop that, Chucky," the man yelled toward the back of the house.

That was an unusual name for dog.

"The little girl used to ride her bike around here," the man added, turning back to Luc.

Used to?

Do they know something the police don't? Why does everyone keep referring to the girl and her stepdad in past tense?

Luc scribbled the information on his notepad.

"The kid used to play around here and sometimes her mother would come to get her bike. She'd leave the bike behind."

Luc thought that was odd that the little girl would ride down there then leave her bike behind. Why would she do that? Was she playing with another kid and forgot? Never mind that, Ms. Morgan never struck him as the kind of mother that would allow her 5-year old to freely roam a new neighborhood.

None of that made much sense. Was she with her stepfather at the time? Or someone else?

"You know the kids love playing with Chucky here. He's a three-legged dog and a nice, fun little fellow," the man said, taking a drink from his beer can.

Oh right, that would explain it. She obviously left her bike to play with the dog. The question was did somebody else watch her while she played with the pet?

"So she loved to play with your dog?" Luc said, jotting down the notes.

"Yep. Her mom's such a nice lady. She'd be so apologetic when she came to get the kid's bike. I told her it's no worries. You know, the kid's welcomed here. I don't mind. There's not that many kids on this street these days. They've all grown up and gone."

"I see." He said, noting more on his notepad.

He thought it was odd that a neighborhood like that didn't have many children there.

He realized that many of the neighbors were much older middle-aged and working age. He figured sometimes maybe the grandkids came over to play. Still, the Morgans only just moved into the neighborhood, probably full of hopes and dreams, and it turned into a street of nightmares.

"Please let us know if you hear anything else or if you remember anything else, sir."

"Will do, Detective. Will do. I hope they catch those criminals who took those nice people away. Just ain't right."

"No, sir. It's not right."

"Sure hope this one has a happy ending."

"Yes let's hope."

It was now 10:40 p.m. As time ticked away, so did hope. But he still held onto hope the girl and her stepdad were safe. Where the hell were they?

Chapter 28

Luc

Detective Luc and his men went door to door on the Garden Green Blvd to interview a few neighbors. Someone must have seen something. Someone must have heard something. Someone knew where that little girl and her step-father were. He just had a gut feeling about it.

He took this case personal. He needed to find that little girl. Fast. This was a whole different matter. Isabell had called earlier in the day and told the officer at the station that her fiancé had gone missing. And as usual, the protocol was that a person could not be declared missing within twenty-four hours to file a report. If they had only known the child was missing too. That would have changed everything.

His mind flashed back to 1997. His wife, Jody, and he were on a trip, a family emergency to visit her dying aunt in Connecticut. They'd left their daughter with their neighbor, Mrs. Lewis, a long-time family friend.

His heart squeezed tightly in his chest at the memory.

They'd received the news, shortly after arriving in Connecticut that his daughter, Jessica, was missing. Missing! Mrs. Lewis had told him she'd been playing with some of the kids in the neighborhood. How could that fucking woman allow an 8-year old to go playing in the neighborhood without adult supervision? Didn't she have an understanding of what the hell "keep an eye on" meant? He hated Mrs. Lewis ever since that day.

He tried hard not to think about it.

That was so many years ago. And now?

Where was Jessica? Was she even alive? Was she somewhere living with someone. He didn't want to think about it. It tore him up inside. But he never stopped looking. Kids sometimes turned up twenty years later after an abduction. That's what kept him going. That one day

120

a lead would turn up. He'd been working with several agencies both nationally and internationally since then.

"You sure you want to handle this case?" his supervisor had asked him. "It's about a missing kid."

"Yeah. I'm sure."

Was he really sure?

He had to find this kid. He wouldn't rest until every corner of the district was searched, every border, every home, every stone turned over. Someone must have seen this kid. There was no way in this quiet little town a grown man and a young child could just go missing.

Without a trace.

Gone without a sign.

How could that be possible?

Luc had seen a lot in his career. Enough to know that there were good neighbors, bad neighbors and neighbors you didn't want to ever live beside.

He'd only just moved to the small town of Ocean Bay Cove. Over a year ago now. He thought he'd change pace from the big city crime. Stuff happened in the small town from time to time, but not like the constant activities of the larger urban dwellings. Still, when stuff did happen, it wasn't any more bearable. Crime was crime. Period.

Most people in small towns tended to look out for each other. But not all the time. He'd seen small town hospitality and he'd also seen small town hostility, especially when outsiders moved in.

"Good evening, ma'am," he said, showing his badge. "Excuse me, but we're searching the area for a missing child."

The woman who opened the door didn't seem alarmed. She was a petite older woman with silver streaks in her hair. She wore round rim glasses. She looked at him as if she didn't understand what he was saying.

A younger man came to the door.

"Hey, everything okay?"

Luc pulled out the picture of Courtney that had been given to him by her mother. "Have you seen this child in the area?"

"They both looked at the picture. The man looked at the older woman and they both exchanged funny glances. Neither seemed alarmed.

"Um. No," he said, shaking his head. Luc looked into this man's eyes. His career was built on being able to tell when people were either lying, bluffing or hiding something. This man was clearly hiding something.

The aroma of marijuana seeped into the air.

He was obviously hiding something. This stuff wasn't even legal, but right now he had to focus his search on the young girl.

"Are you sure? Take a good look." He offered the photo. The man barely looked at it.

"No, man. Haven't seen....haven't seen the kid."

"They live in the area."

"Yeah, I know. They moved across the street. N-nice family. I mostly see the woman though."

"Have you noticed anything strange at all?"

He thought for a moment. Then he shook his head. "No, officer. Haven't noticed anything...um...no."

"May I come in to take a look?"

He paused for a moment. Then opened his door wider. If he were hiding something or someone, he probably would have hesitated.

The officer looked around and gave the area a good scan for any signs of anything suspicious. He didn't see or feel anything odd going on there. He didn't think they would need a search warrant or anything.

"Thank you, sir. Ma'am. Please let us know if you remember anything or if you've seen anything suspicious."

"Uh, yeah...um...sure."

The woman said nothing. "Are you all right, ma'am?"

"Si." The woman's voice was strong. She obviously understood some English.

"Have a good day, ma'am."

He left the house feeling dejected. He'd never felt that way before. Not like this. Was it because this case involved a missing child? Like the one case he could never solve involving his own daughter?

He tried to convince himself that was not the case. He was just tired.

But one thing he missed about the big city was cameras. They were everywhere. People didn't trust as much in the urban dwellings or larger cities. They installed cameras over their garages of their homes. The buildings were loaded with them. In the small towns, especially ones like Ocean Bay Cove in Cove County, filled with older Victorian homes and dwellings, the thought never occurred to them that it would be necessary. Nobody had cameras installed over their garages or on their doors.

Damn it.

The trust in the community might work against them in this case. If he were in any big city, he'd immediately have asked everyone to check their security cameras. That would have been a cinch. They would have been way further ahead on their case. The security footage could have shown which direction the man took with the child and if any cars had followed them. It was obvious they could have been abducted together while he'd walked the girl to the daycare. But by whom? Who would do this in this small town? Who knew about that envelope?

Someone knew the guy. There must have been a vendetta. Perhaps his past caught up with him?

But Ms. Morgan truly believed her fiancé was a good guy, and something bad must have happened to him and the girl—even though he'd lied about going to the gym.

Luc wiped his brow as he headed to the next neighbor's house. Something told him this case was going to be unlike any other he'd ever worked on.

Chapter 29

10:55 p.m.

I pulled back the curtain to take a peek outside at all the commotion on the street. I slowly took a sip of coffee, slurping it, savoring the flavor as it went down my throat. I couldn't believe all the excitement over little Courtney and her step-daddy.

As if watching a good game on the TV, I was enjoying this. This was one of the most clever games yet. Look at the cops on the street combing the area, going from door to door. I shook my head and grinned.

One thing's for sure. They would never in a million years guess where Courtney and her step-daddy were.

Never in a million years.

I was the only person who knew where they were—but they'd never guess.

Chapter 30

Luc

Frustration ripped through Luc as he sat at his desk at the police station. He'd been working a double shift and it was beginning to fray his nerves, though not as much as the missing persons case. This baffled him. He didn't have a clue. Was he losing his touch? He was psychologically spent, drained. Maybe he just needed to catch a few zzzs. His men were still on the case, hunting for the missing girl and her stepfather.

Getting ready to fill out his report, he glanced at his notes. He realized that everybody was different. People were like their fingerprints, no two were alike.

Still the whole case was beginning to eat away at his nerves. He was obsessed over finding the little girl safe and sound. Where could they have gone? Time made a big difference. The more time ticked away, the less chance there was for a happy ending.

"You know what?" he said to his colleague near by, at his desk, shuffling through some files.

"What?"

He drank the rest of his coffee.

"We found out the woman has some issues."

"Issues?"

"Yeah, her aunt said she suffered from depression and had some mental health issues. Not that it should matter because anyone can be sick, but I'm wondering if that upset the guy. Did the guy get fed up and leave with the kid?"

"But that makes little sense."

"Yeah, she seems like a nice lady though. I'm just trying to figure things out. She did seem a bit out of it. Of course, she's missing her kid. A lot of the neighbors say the same thing, that she's a bit strange, talks to herself a lot. Is she telling us everything? Was the guy stressing her out? She told me he's waiting for them to get married so he could get his papers and be legal here and get a job."

"Do you think that's something to do with the kidnapping or the missing persons situation?"

He looked thoughtful. "Wish I knew. There's something off here and I just can't quite put my finger on it. Damn, that drives me crazy."

"Don't get crazy on us now," his colleague teased.

"That's our most valuable asset."

"What is?"

"Our mind."

"Your mind?"

"Once you lose your mind that's it. You're not even aware of anything. "

"Okay, Mr. Freud."

"No, seriously, people need to protect their mind more than anything else. You don't want to lose that."

"No, you don't."

"One thing is for sure, you can't control what happens to you, but you can control what happens *inside* of you."

"You know we've checked out the neighbor Mrs. D before. Her daughter and husband were driving her crazy. Next thing you know, they disappear."

"She said they went out west."

"Yeah, but out west where? Somewhere in the basement or the garden?"

"We couldn't get a court order to excavate. There's no reason to believe they're dead. I mean no one's reported them missing. They'd told their workplaces they were planning to split."

"How convenient for Mrs. D."

"Come on now. We have no proof."

"But history could repeat itself. The neighbors keep saying Isabell Morgan's a bit off, talks to herself and all. What if she's crazy. For some reason the guy's giving her trouble and she makes him vanish. That brown envelope marked *Do Not Open Until September 25th* is pretty convenient. Who else would know about it but them?"

"But the kid? What about the kid? She loves that little girl. No one's disputed that."

Luc perished the thought that Morgan could have had anything to do with it. Though they'd managed much worse cases in the big cities, he just didn't think this was the case here.

Isabell Morgan was a troubled soul. He could just sense it. Then again, her fiancé had told her he'd been working in the basement and it seemed as if he hadn't done much. Was that a point of contention? Was she really upset that she found out he hadn't fixed the basement step as he'd said and almost fell and broke her neck because of it?

Luc had to look at all angles. But most importantly he had to find the little girl before it was too late, and her stepfather.

He decided he'd talk to the stress disorder experts at the local college and after this was all over he was going to suggest that Isabell Morgan speak to someone. He had a gut feeling that Isabell's situation would be far from resolved—even after they found her daughter. If they ever found her daughter.

He thought about it as he took another swig of coffee. According to the records they found of her online, Isabell Morgan was a spelling bee champion. She also graduated summa cum laude in philosophy and history. In fact, she had two bachelor's degrees and a Masters. Not bad. She was well-educated and used to be involved in the community, she had several volunteer positions with various organizations back in Ontario and in the United States. She'd lost a lot along the way, including her confidence. She'd lost her job, her parents, and came out of an abusive relationship. At the hands of an abusive boyfriend. That was a lot for one person to take. They'd found a lot of information through internal records.

It wasn't unusual in a case like this to check out everyone close to the child as much as possible to find out what could have happened.

"You think the guy took the kid and ran off?"

"That would be pretty stupid. I think something happened to them all right. Don't know if he was involved."

"How so?"

He thought about the irony of the situation during the investigation he went upstairs to look into the closet and saw that Erik and Courtney still had their clothes there.

He even checked out Isabell's closet. All her clothes were there. What he didn't do was look into Isabell's closet, not her physical closet but the closet that could have skeletons in it. The skeletons of the past. The burdens she was carrying.

There was some contradictory information surrounding her mother and father's death. It was quite possible that someone from her father's past caught up with her. She'd displayed too much information on social media about her whereabouts. It was a long shot but it looked as if someone followed her out there.

"Dan," Luc called out.

"Yes, boss."

"I want you to try to find out which neighbor on that street moved there recently."

"Yes, boss."

The rookie left and went to his computer database.

Something wasn't adding up. Something was off n that neighborhood.

Something was missing all right, not just the kid and the stepdaddy.

"You know something?" he said.

"What is it, boss?"

"I've interviewed countless neighbors on that little street there. *Somebody* is lying. And I want to know why?"

11:00 p.m.

"So you're saying the only eye-witness might be a parrot?" Luc's supervisor, Sandy, arched her brow, her tone dubious. She'd just gotten in for her graveyard shift and had been briefed about the case. Not that she needed much briefing since it had made the local news.

"Not saying that at all. But anything's possible. The parrot obviously saw something. Now what would make a parrot say look? Was the parrot about to say look out?"

"Who knows? I've heard parrots have the powerful ability to mimic humans. But to warn them? That's one advanced bird."

"It sure is," he said, gulping down the rest of his coffee.

Why did he have a sick feeling the neighbors weren't being honest about everything?

"Sir, I got the image you wanted," a rookie interrupted them. "You said it was urgent."

"Yeah, thanks, Roger."

Luc went over to his computer and glanced at the blue coat that Courtney wore in the picture. It looked like a very expensive coat. Her mother certainly gave her the best, but could she have afforded it? According to the reports they'd gotten, she'd just cashed in her parents' life insurance. It was just enough to pay off their debts and to purchase the house, but it didn't leave her with much money to live off of for too long. Apparently, she was sending Courtney to daycare so she could go look for work. Erik was supposed be looking for work too. They moved to the small town to save money from living in a big city, but were they running to a new freedom or running *from* something?

He glanced at the coat again. There was something about that coat that was bothering him.

He called the lab.

"Yes sir."

"I need you to do something for me. Could you zoom in on the background image of the girl with the blue coat."

"Yes, boss."

Luc was a man of detail and he knew there must be something in that coat that would give him more information. Nothing was as clean as it seemed.

It wasn't whether a person was lying, but whether they believed what they were saying that made a difference.

For some folks, certain things or events could be real in their own minds.

He shook his head at the irony of the situation. He'd relocated to Ocean Bay Cove for a light break from the heavy crime-ridden inner cities. Boy, had he been wrong. This was going to be the case that would change him, if it didn't kill him.

* * *

Luc glanced again at the screen of the computer, scrutinizing the data he picked up the phone. "Did you find anything, Steve?"

"I was just about to call you, sir. I checked like you said, but nothing suspicious came up on the date, September 25th."

"You sure?"

"I'm sure, sir."

"I find it strange the woman was told not to open the brown envelope until September 25th of this year. I'm pretty sure it must have something to do with some statute of limitation."

"Really?"

"Just a hunch. Keep looking."

"Will do, Boss."

"You know what's very strange?" Luc said to the rookie sitting on the next desk over from the left.

"Yes, sir?"

"Erik has no fingerprints."

"Fingerprints, sir?" The rookie looked at him as if he were crazy.

"Digital fingerprints," he clarified.

"Digital fingerprints?"

Now the rookie was beginning to sound like that couple's parrot. He really wasn't in the mood to have every word imitated right now.

"Yes, digital fingerprint. Whether people like to believe it or not, everyone's got a digital fingerprint online. Within the database of a government organization or social media, even their address is online on Google maps."

"I don't get what you're trying to say, sir."

"This guy doesn't seem to have a digital fingerprint, at least not one that he wants us to know about. According to Isabell, he seems like this wonderful guy, but is Erik who he says he is? He played football in Los Angeles back in high school, but that was it. He vanished since then."

"Not everybody likes to be on social media, sir. Unless he changed his name."

"Or his identity since then."

"That's true."

"There's something about this guy I think he's hiding from his future wife. It's as if he eliminated all of his ID's, his bank accounts... how can a person manage that in this digital age? Unless..."

"Unless what, Sir?"

"Unless he was *trying* to disappear."

Chapter 31

12:10 a.m.

Luc was nodding off at his desk when the call came in. Adrenaline coursed through him. Did they find the kid? Did they find the father? Were they both safe? God, he hoped so. He didn't always pray, but right now, he was praying for a miracle to this case. A happy ending.

"You found them?"

"No, sir. Well, not yet."

"Not yet? What do you mean not yet?"

"Sir, she left."

"What? Who left?"

"Isabell Morgan, sir. She left the house."

"I thought you were supposed to be looking out for anything suspicious. When did she leave?"

"About five minutes ago. Johnson's on the case. He went for a coffee break and when he came back, she was gone."

"Shit. What do you have?"

"Looks as if the kidnapper contacted her and asked her to meet him."

"Good. Anyone tracking?"

"Yes, sir. We're keeping a close surveillance."

Luc got up and grabbed his jacket, throwing it on, fastening his holster. He needed to get there before she does. Before she got herself killed.

Chapter 32

Lake Mceuelek, Border of Ocean Bay Cove, NS
12:10 a.m.
Isabell

Isabell's pulse pounded in her throat as she sat on the passenger seat of her neighbor, Dillon's, car. Her stomach tightened into knots. She knew she should have told the cops about the next text messages, but she didn't want anything to happen to her daughter and to Erik. She had nothing to lose and everything to gain.

He said he'd kill them if she came with the cops. She squeezed her eyes shut and felt pain in her chest at the thought.

No.

She couldn't allow anything like that to happen.

Dillon had come by to offer her some help if she ever needed it well so she called him. He came over. He was always friendly and helpful. She told him about the messages and he said he'd drive her to the location at River Drive. It was an abandoned lot with a cottage and a barn.

At least she was with a neighbor. What could go wrong? The police knew him, he wouldn't do anything foolish.

Her aunt was still sound asleep. She didn't want to wake her up. She'd bring Courtney back home safely and that would be that.

When they pulled up at the location specified from the E text message. The area wasn't very well lit. She was beginning to have regrets.

Your daughter will be dead if you come with cops. Drop off the brown envelope and leave.

She played over the message in her mind, her thoughts racing dangerously at the possible scenarios if she didn't comply.

She only hoped she wasn't putting her neighbor's life into danger too. He didn't seem too bothered.

"Well, we're here," he said, stifling a yawn

"Sorry to do this to you."

"Hey, no worries. That's what neighbors are for."

"You're very kind, you know that."

She got out of the car and closed the door. She looked around. The roar of the ocean waves beat against the rock. There were some lights illuminated. Some boats were tied to the dock and rocking from side to side. Where were they?

"Hello?" she called out.

She tightened her grip on the large brown envelope. She had Courtney's plush toy in her other hand. She was determined to give it back to her little girl.

"I don't see anyone..." She turned back to the car, but Dillon was gone.

"Dillon! Dillon!" Her eyes widened in shock.

What the hell just happened?

Now she knew this had been a bad mistake.

Had they taken Dillon too?

She reached into her purse for her cell phone to call the cops, but it was missing.

"Looking for this?" A man in the shadow walked slowly towards her from the barn. He held out a device in his hand.

What the—-

"Who are you?"

When he came into the light. She saw who it was and her body ran cold.

Chapter 33

Isabell

"Sorry, doll, but I had to do this. By the way, you should've listened to the cops." Dillon's grin was evil, wide and void of emotions. His eyes were dark and cold. Why hadn't she seen that before?

"You? Why? Where's my baby? Where's Erik?"

"Oh, come on now. You don't remember me?"

"No. I don't."

"Your Daddy and I went into business together and he stole my idea then made a killing on it with some online pyramid. Embezzled funds from some dead guy who'd partnered with us before he died and wired the funds to a Swiss bank account. His estate went looking for the funds. That was ten years ago."

"Ten years?" she echoed, filled with fury. "You're waiting for the statute of limitation to run out so you can't be prosecuted?"

"Yeah, something like that."

"You're wrong. You can still go down for that. It's just plain wrong."

"If they catch me. I'll be long gone by then—much like your mind," he grinned. "By the way that no-name brand smart speaker was a good idea. It's from a company I helped get started. Until I got kicked out of it. Anyway, it came in handy. That's how I was able to track you, darling. I managed to override the system and get into it. I knew you'd be coming to Ocean Bay Cove, so I made sure to move back here. Convenient, huh?"

"You're poisonous." Shock ripped through her body.

'Like your old man was, the backstabbing bastard. He once asked me to drive him to the hospital so he could visit you. I knew you had severe problems. Didn't know how badly though. Glad it worked out now."

"What are you...you talking about?"

"You're all crazy. You and your family. I want the bank details in that package."

"You can have it. I wouldn't want anything to do with dirty money. I'd rather be clean and honest."

"And broke?" he laughed.

"You can't put a price on a clear conscious and peace of mind, Dillon. Rich folks without peace have taken their own lives."

He scoffed.

"Listen, I just want my daughter back. Please." She pleaded with him.

"Don't worry, I wouldn't hurt them. You can have them back once I get the envelope and what's mine. I tied them up nice and snug. They're in the cottage."

She pulled out the envelope out of her bag. "I want to see them first."

"First, the envelope."

She hesitated at first. "I need proof they're still...alive."

He paused. "Oh, come on now. You think I'd hurt your little girl? What kind of monster do you think I am? Your father, now he was a monster. I was happy to hear you were moving out east here on the coast. That worked out great. My daddy and your daddy bought properties out here back in the day. Again, he left my father with the bill. Anyway, I came out here. Glad you did too or you would have ended up like your old man and your mammy. Sorry about her though."

Her eyes widened in shock.

"*You*. You killed my parents." Her heart thudded in her chest. Her limbs felt weak. How was she going to get away now?

"Can't prove it," he said.

"Daddy trusted you." She almost pleaded with him while her eyes darted to see if there was an escape, a way out.

"Trust? You call that trust? That was my fucking idea and he stole it from me. Took all those contacts and scammed those people. Where was my cut?"

"Your cut's coming soon. And it won't be anything you could have imagined." Her voice hardened. Why was she getting hard all of a sudden? He could very well kill her. No one would ever find her.

Be careful who you trust.

Detective Luc's voice thrust into her mind like an energy force. He hadn't been referring to Erik at all. He'd been referring to Dillon. Dillon was the one she should have been leery of from the get go.

"Where's Courtney? Where's Erik?"

"They're here safe. Once you give me the envelope."

Her breathing was labored.

Never negotiate with a criminal.

She knew deep down he could very well get the envelope and kill all that was dear to her. What was she going to do?

Everything happened so fast, she heard sirens and cruisers on the scene, the police stormed in and everything else was a blur...

Chapter 34

Luc

"You okay?" Luc asked Isabell.

She was visibly shaken. She hugged herself, dazed. He was glad he got to her in time.

"Courtney!" she exclaimed. "Erik," she said, breathing hard, panting. Her eyes were wide with shock. "Erik and Courtney are in the cottage. He....he told me he tied them up."

Luc wasted no time. He got up and went over to Dillon as the officer read him his rights then proceeded to take him into the back of the police cruiser.

"Where's the kid? Where's the fiancé?"

Dillon gave Luc a strange look. His eyes were wild. He could just imagine what was going on in his mind. Time was running out. Did Courtney and Erik have enough oxygen? Were they going to die soon if he didn't get to them?

"Listen," Luc told him, his voice stern. "You'll do time for kidnapping, but murder? You'll never see the light of day."

Dillon slowly turned his head over to the area where a cottage stood. It looked abandoned. Dillon then looked at Isabell and a smirk crept onto his dry lips. "They're in that cottage over there."

"Hold right here," Luc instructed the other officer. He was going to make sure they were alive and well before he allowed them to drive off with Dillon. He also wanted to make sure Dillon wasn't leading them on another wild goose chase.

"I'm coming with you," Isabell said.

"No. You stay right here."

"I'm coming with you!" Her voice rose in alarm. Her eyes were wild. She was determined.

"Isabell," he said, his voice softening slightly. He knew these situations didn't always end up well to say it nicely. Sometimes what he discovered was so horrific it gave him nightmares. Nightmares he had to go on antidepressants for a year to get out of his mind. And even then, he'd suffered from post-traumatic stress syndrome, much like Isabell from what happened to her in her own horrific past. But he didn't want her to suffer any more emotional damage than she'd already suffered. It wouldn't be fair to her.

He hesitated for a moment. A shadow of doubt crossed his mind. Could she handle this? Her expression was telling him that she was not going to stay back. It was not subject to negotiation.

"The lady wants to go," Dillon said with a smirk. "Let her go."

"You have the right to remain *silent*! Use it!" Luc yelled out between clenched teeth. Fury rose inside him. Was Dillon taunting him? What the hell happened to the little girl and her would-be step daddy?

"Fine, you can come. But you need to stay behind me."

She hugged herself eagerly, following him to the cottage where the truth would be revealed.

Chapter 35

Dillon

Busted. Dillon was caught. There was no turning back now. The question was, should he have told them what *really* happened to Erik and Courtney?

Nah. They didn't deserve it. Cops. He didn't care too much for them. Then again, they were on the opposite side of the law, weren't they?

Time. He always thought he needed more time to get all the money in the world. Now, time was something he wouldn't have. It was something he'd be doing.

Shit.

Still, he wished he could be there to see the look on Detective Luc's fucking face when he opened the door of the cottage. What was he going to do to Dillon then? Nothing. He was in police custody. He knew his rights. There wasn't shit he could do to him and he knew it. This case was high profile now. A little girl missing and her daddy-to-be.

Ha.

Dillon laughed internally.

You'll never guess in a million years where Courtney and Erik are.

He watched them, eyes narrowed as they walked up the stone steps to the cottage, about to open the door to a horror they could never see coming. A different kind of horror.

In fact, he felt giddy inside. Shit. This was going to work out in his favor. He always won in the end. Her fucking father tried to screw around with him and shaft him out of his share of the money and he got what he deserved. Then his daughter tried to play him. Well, he was sure she knew what she was doing. Still, once they saw Erik and Courtney. Once the media saw what he did to them, he'd get off by reason of insanity.

Reason of insanity.

That was an understatement wasn't it?

He looked at Isabell.

She was a fucking mess. They thought he was insane. She was a real shit mess of a beautiful woman.

He watched as they slowly opened the cottage door, guns drawn as if expecting a trap or danger. He wished he could be there to see how they were going to find Courtney and Erik. All tied up...and...

Chapter 36

Luc

The officer beside Luc kicked open the front door to the cottage. The place was dark. The officers had their guns positioned and followed protocol and procedure upon entering. Combing the area swiftly looking for signs of anyone.

Was this a trap?

Sweat beaded on Luc's forehead. His heart raced. This place was in no condition for any human being. The abandoned place was termite infested and covered in cobwebs and dust. That Dillon better not have led them on a wild good chase.

He had ordered the other officer to keep Isabell back, just in case.

"Hello," he said. He thought he heard commotion coming from behind. He jumped back when a raccoon hurried across.

Raccoon.

That wasn't a good sign.

He could imagine them being tied up huddled in a corner somewhere.

"Hello," he called out again. He looked into another room where the door was hanging off the hinges.

He then saw another door had been bolted shut. He listened at the door. Nothing. He then tried the door then kicked it open with his right foot.

His body tensed. His jaw fell open.

What the—

Chapter 37

12:45 a.m.

Isabell

Isabell could wait no longer. "I need to go in there!"

"Wait here, ma'am," an officer beside her tried to motion to her to keep back.

"But that's my daughter in there. She needs me. Please let me go."

She heard the officer receive a call on his radio. When he went to fetch it, she made her way inside.

"Ma'am, please..."

She ran inside the cottage and made a beeline into the room where she saw Detective Luc standing at the doorway, the look of horror on his face.

Oh, no. Was it too late? Were they...dead?

She pushed passed him, knocking him over as he lost his balance and he didn't even try to hold her back. He just looked paralyzed with shock.

Luc

Detective Luc Renald struggled to get back up after his limbs buckled under him. His eyes captured the scene before him. In all his twenty years on the force, he thought he'd seen everything, but *this*?

His brain was unable to process the scene before him. He couldn't grasp what was in front of him.

This shook the very core of his stability.

He would never look at people the same way again.

How could he?

He needed to retire now.

He would never be the same again after this case. That much was true...

Isabell reached over to hug her daughter?

"Baby," she cried over and over again. Her voice climbed with emotion. "Mommy's here, darling. I'm here. Erik I'm so glad you two are all right. I was so worried about you."

Luc tried to process what was going on. What the fuck was going on? Had this woman suffered a breakdown?

There he saw two chairs with ropes tied around them but no one there. Only some old pillows. And when he said old, they were worn and filthy. But that's not what the woman saw. She quickly untied the ropes on both chairs. Then she hugged herself as if a child was in her arms. Then she turned slightly to her left and patted her shoulder as if someone was holding her.

Fuck.

Either she was losing her mind, or he was.

"Call the suspect back in here," Detective Luc radioed to the other officer, still dazed in shock.

Then he paused.

His mind rushed back over the past twenty-four hours. The neighbors' eye witness accounts. "I always saw the little girl...well, her bike anyway."

His mouth was still open in shock. His heart muscles contracted with a force so great, he thought the only arrest going on today was going to be a cardiac arrest—his own.

"Ma'am?" he finally said, dazed. He watched her eyes filled with emotion. She was happy. Her emotions exhibited the same emotion he'd seen on family members who find their loved ones safe and sound, alive after an ordeal. He could feel the energy in the room. It was real. Palpable.

Voices haunted his mind as his thoughts travelled down a whirlwind of clues he'd missed along this path...

"Never did see them. I only saw the girl's bike...and the man's shoes at the door..."

"She was always buying her little girl things. Never saw the kid, but I knew she must be the luckiest kid around here. Her mommy picked up all the fun toys a little girl could have..." the store owner had said.

"She's a strange woman," the couple at number 75 on the street had told him. "She's always out talking to herself. She was at the park once, talking to herself pretending to be talking to a kid...the other kids looked at her and laughed...they called her weird...they saw her alone pretending to talk to someone that was smaller than she was...But it's as if someone's with her. Now I don't believe in ghosts but...well, you know, we try to keep to ourselves. We also have a cousin back in Wisconsin—crazy as a bat from hell, but I suppose there's always one in every family. So we try not to judge. But she's always wheeling that little pink bike down the street as if a kid is on it. Then she leaves the bike wherever then walks to the park as if she's holding a child's hand...only nothing is there. Just the air. Bizarre."

"Yes, she called the daycare and told us she just moved into the neighborhood and she had a five year old," Sheena, the daycare supervisor had told him. "We were supposed to meet her for the first time today...She was supposed to bring in all the girl's documents and fill in some forms...but no one showed up...then she called and asked if her fiancé had picked up the kid...we were like what kid? She never showed up..."

"So glad that she finally moved on with her life," her aunt Sarah's voice echoed in his head, "After her crazy ass ex beat her up so badly, they told her she'd never be able to conceive or have kids...imagine that! They told her that she would never be able to have kids because of that violent bastard she was dating...but I'm so glad she proved them wrong. I wish I'd be around when her child was born. I wish I got a chance to meet her...I haven't spoken to the family in so long. Seven years. I never even knew Isabell was pregnant...."

One thing was for sure. The mind could play one hell of a trick on you if you weren't careful.

We see what we think we should see.

The clues were there all along and he'd missed it. Something was missing all right. Something *was* missing...

Her mind.

Chapter 38

Luc

When they left the cottage, Luc had called for the crisis team to come in to see to Isabell. He'd also contacted her auntie. He tried to tell Isabell that no one was there. But he had to tread carefully. The officers exchanged glances. They had to redirect her gently to reality but in a careful way. She'd already been traumatized.

"My daughter would like a glass of water, please. She's thirsty," Isabell said. Nothing in his twenty-year history with the force could bring him to tears. But his one caused him to choke with emotion. He was hoping so badly this case would have a happy ending. But did it? Was she not happy? She might appear to be happy or believe she was happy, but there was another sad state of affairs going on there. Her life. Her reality. The lines between her delusions and reality were blurring fast. So fast, he didn't know if she could ever get back.

But that brought him to another question.

Dillon.

What the fuck was Dillon playing at?

"You'll never guess where they are," he said with a grin. "They're locked up here," he gestured to his head, rolling his eyes upward. "In the space between her ears. Between her good ear and her bad ear." The grin grew wider.

He knew all along, didn't he?

He'd been watching her and figured it early enough. They had traced a call where he spoke to his would-be kidnapping accomplice and told him to hold off, he was doing this one alone. Change in development. Yeah, a change in development all right.

His men had already confirmed that according to the diary notes they found on Dillon's property, he'd discovered her mental illness was so severe and decided to change plans. He had searched all sorts of information on cases about severe cases of patients who suffered from

Delusion Disorder. Then he'd managed to look up stuff on her own battles with mental illness especially after her parents' death and her ex's incarceration for what he'd done to her.

He was playing up to her charade, her delusion to get close to her to give him the passcodes to her father's accounts so that he could steal the funds her father supposedly owed him.

Crazy bastard.

If Luc could wipe that cocky smirk off Dillon's face, he would.

Sick bastard played them all. He knew about Isabell's illness and took advantage of her. But what was he going to do afterward? What had he been planning to do to Isabell? Detective Luc didn't want to dwell on that right now.

He had one of a hell of a report to fill out soon. Not to mention addressing the media.

What was he going to say about this massive hunt for a child that didn't exist, except in the woman's mind?

Chapter 39

Luc

Isabell had suffered enough torment and abuse all her life. The last thing he would want was for her to go through more. Once stuff got on the Internet, it stayed there forever. He had to protect her at all costs.

What could he say to address this sensitive situation?

Of course the clues were there all along. How could Luc have missed it? Erik was embedded so deeply in Isabell's life in her soul. Just like the characters in the novel. He became part of her. And nobody could shake that vision of reality. Everything was new in her mind. Her own coping mechanism. A very severe mental breakdown. Her visual senses became wrapped up in the solution. That she could see nothing else but what she wanted to see. She believed what she wanted to believe.

The crisis team came by to assist beheld her as she held onto her daughter that was real in her mind and her fiancé that existed only in her mind in her world.

"Can I get you anything?" Luc turned to Isabell one more time. They were about to take her to the local hospital.

"Yes. Could you please take my keys and go to my home. Courtney's favorite doll. I left it there."

Luc looked at the crisis team nurse and then back to Isabell.

The woman gave him the go-ahead. It was probably best to gently redirect her back to reality but not to force her right now.

Support. They had to be as supportive as they could to her. Her family may not be real but what just happened to her *was* real.

She was kidnapped by this lunatic criminal. She needed all the support that she could get. She'd also been badly abused and beaten by her ex-boyfriend. That was real. The traumatic effects were real to her.

Was this a severe case of post-traumatic stress disorder?

He took the keys and reassured her he'd get what she needed. Thankfully her aunt was still there. He'd have to speak to her. How was he going to break the news to her?

Luc drove back to Garden Green Blvd. in a daze. He was questioning reality and what was real and what wasn't.

When he pulled up at number forty-seven it all came back to him. Everybody's testimony even the neighbor at number eighty.

Of course the neighbor at number eighty was an attention seeker. He'd seen it all before. Even in accidents where you had ten witness testimonies and each person would see a different angle of the accident.

Sometimes people saw what they wanted to see. Sometimes after a celebrity died people came out of the woodwork and made up stories about being with this person of interest. This was a big deal a little girl and her step-daddy going missing. Everybody wanted a piece of the action.

So they all made up and believed a version of how sweet the guy was. The neighbor at number eighty said that he was so kind and even offered to cut her grass one day. Really?

Yeah he'd cut her grass all right?

Shit.

Why didn't he see it coming?

When Luc finally arrived, her aunt half-asleep had let him in and then went back to the sofa to crash out. She was obviously tired. He went into the living room and there was the book that he'd seen before that bothered him and now he knew why.

He picked up the book and horror crept inside him.

The Billionaire Daddy and the Secretary Fall In Love. It was a romance novel. He turned the book over and looked at the description of the story. He was compelled to do this for some reason.

He read the blurb.

His eyes wide open for the first time seeing the truth. Seeing the effect of mental breakdown and abuse. What it could do to a person.

God Almighty.

The description read:

> *Meet Erik Joneson, twenty-nine, the handsome billionaire*
> *Prince who lives undercover in the big city and is looking for*
> *someone to take good care of his daughter, Courtney, though*
> *what she really needs is a suitable mother.*

Detective Luc felt sick inside. For the first time chills slithered down his spine. Goosebumps sprung up all over his arms in and the hair on his neck stood up to attention.

He felt his lungs burn with pain.

How could he have missed this?

This poor beautiful woman who'd been so badly abused in her past not only lost herself in this book, she lost her world in this book.

He read a few passages that described Erik as being six-foot four inches, handsome, well-built and a tattoo on his right arm.

Good God! She'd imagined the whole thing! She'd brought him out of the story and into her own life.

He hated her ex-boyfriend for abusing her now even more than ever. But he refused to believe that her story ended here. He knew the people could recover from the greatest of ailments. He really believed in it.

But right now he was going to need some serious debriefing.

Why did he have a sick feeling that the story was not going to end here?

There was more to the story. And he was determined to get down to the truth.

Right now, how were they going to tell Isabell that the beautiful parts of her life were only an illusion, while the chaotic parts were real?

Her aunt Sarah's face was white as a ghost now when Luc had woken her up and told her. He'd told her they'd taken Isabell to the Ocean Bay General Hospital Psych ward.

"My niece has always had a vivid imagination. A very strong imagination." Her aunt Sarah said.

Vivid imagination? That was an understatement...

Chapter 40

Luc

Luc had already spoken to Sarah Morgan, Isabell's aunt, who was just as shaken up as he was about the whole situation. She was already at the Ocean Bay Cove Hospital Mental Health Ward with her niece now.

Sarah hadn't seen or spoken to Isabell in over seven years so she'd assumed that when Isabell got in contact with her what she was saying about her life was true. She hadn't posted any pictures on social media, though Sarah wasn't on social media. She was horrified despite all the signs in the house that Erik and Courtney had been part of Isabell's delusional disorder. She was shaken to realize that the kidnapping wasn't a part of her disorder, but she had in fact been watched and preyed upon by a neighbor for other reasons.

"You know what really gets me?" Luc said to his associate at the police station.

"What?"

"The neighbors. Were they in on it too? Why did they play along with the idea that Courtney was real?"

"They didn't. We did."

"Come again?" she said, arching a brow.

"I went back and interviewed some of the neighbors after the fact."

"And?"

"I just realized how deadly preconceived ideas could be. Whatever we believe, we could alter facts in our mind to agree with our beliefs, fair or unfair. Right or wrong. We see a person from a certain culture walking down the street. We might think he's going to work? Or looking for trouble, or whatever depending on our beliefs that might not have anything to do with reality."

"I see. But what does this have to do with the child?"

"We told them a kid was missing. So they talked about how the kid used to play on the street or near their house. Why? Because they saw the bike."

"Oh, right. That little pink training wheels bike."

"Exactly. Isabell would take the bike down the street as if walking with her child on a bike."

She shook her head in pity, sorrow filled her eyes. "How awful it must have been for her."

"For anyone who might have caught a glimpse of her doing that, yeah, but in her own mind, her daughter was on that bike. In any event, for what reason, I have no idea, but she used to just leave the bike wherever and go take her kid, her alleged kid, to the park and walk the rest of the way. In her mind, that was happening. Now her neighbors would say they would see the kid's bike. We believed in our heads there really was a kid. There was no reason in our mind to disbelieve Isabell. Then the daycare assumed the child existed because the mother called and told them they'd just moved to the area and wanted to enroll her kid in the daycare."

"Right," she said, nodding thoughtfully.

"So everything that happened, we missed any clues because there was no reason to believe the child didn't exist. Until I picked up on a few things. But even then I refused to listen to reason. I still assumed."

"You wanted to avenge."

"Yeah, I did. My own kid went missing. I'll never be able to rest until I know what really happened to her."

"I'm so sorry about that."

"I wonder what she would be doing now. It tore my wife and I apart. I wonder if that's why she left me. She went sleeping around. I worked myself to numbness. Working every second of the day, double shifts. Everything. Anything so I wouldn't have to think about it. We all cope in different ways, I suppose. For Isabell, having been a victim of domestic abuse and being told she may never conceive again, because of her ex boyfriend's attack on her, was all too much to bear. Not to mention whatever was going on with her father. She slid into a safe world, a world in her mind that was safer. She brought the characters of a romance novel to life and they behaved in her mind the way loved ones *should* behave to her."

"That's right. You said you saw romance novels scattered about the place."

"Yes. And her massive bookshelf. In this day and age of digital books, never thought I'd see a house with tons of bookshelves. They were the only things unpacked. Which brings me to another observation. The fact that the boxes were still unpacked. No wonder. She had no help. She thought she did, but she didn't. Then there was the basement stairs. No wonder the place was a mess," he said, raking his fingers through his hair in disbelief. "There wasn't anyone working down there. It was only in her head."

"But then your report said the neighbor, Mrs. D heard banging."

"That's just it. Remember I told you she was strange."

"Oh, right."

"Exactly. She's another case. Isabell told me Mrs. D said it was good that she found a neighbor just like her. Well, no wonder. Mrs. D believes her stuffed toys are real. She went over to Isabell's home and found her talking to her make belief daughter and immediately felt right at home. She too suffers from a bit of delusion. She told Isabell they were alike, but Isabell didn't get it at the time."

"Wonder if she does now. Wonder what's going through her mind right now."

"Me too." His voice was quiet, practically inaudible.

"Wow. Unbelievable."

"What's unbelievable is how powerful the brain is, the power of the imagination. And her auntie Sarah had been so estranged from the family for the past seven years, shutting off all communication with them and not being on social media or anything, she had no idea what was going on in Isabell's life. She knew she had suffered depression earlier in her life, but not even she thought this whole, charade, for lack of a better word, could have been possible."

"I see."

"I wanted to find this girl so badly, I missed the clues that she might not really exist."

"But what about the picture?"

"That's it." He grabbed the picture from his desk, still in shock. "I knew something was off about it and that someone must be lying to me. The trouble I had was with the coat. It was from this designer Ofron. They were hot back in the 1990's. The picture was taken outside of the Lecenze Mall in Caledon County. That mall was demolished by the late nineties. Long before the girl was born."

"What?"

"Exactly. And the coat brand, Ofron, hadn't been around in forever. I knew I recognized it. This is a picture of Isabell when she was younger which was why I didn't think much of the resemblance. I knew the era was off though. Sure, it's a color photo, but there was something last century about it. Just couldn't figure it out."

"We see what we think we should see."

"What we want to see."

He gazed again at the photo in disbelief. How did he manage to miss the clues, the signs?

"Though I admit, Isabell was good. The way things worked out was brilliant. Very convincing. And not to mention the neighbor, Dillon."

Dillon had obviously changed his mind about killing her when he saw she was stark crazy and talking to herself—pretending to be living with her family. That was the reason why he decided to call off the kidnapping and murder and decided to pretend to kidnap her fake daughter and fake fiancé instead, toying with her mind, trying to blackmail her into giving him the brown envelope—the stuff he needed to clean out her finances that her father left her with. And he saw that it was working. He'd researched her disorder online and carefully watched her to see how far he could go.

"Dillon threw us off completely by going so far as to lie about seeing her fiancé and daughter and that he'd been watching her fiancé. When I asked him certain questions about Erik, though, I found it strange that he didn't know Erik had a tattoo on his right arm. A very noticeable one. For someone, who supposedly had this Erik character under surveillance, he really tripped up there."

"Glad you caught it, Detective."

"Wished I'd caught it sooner."

Chapter 41

Ocean Bay Cove General Hospital, Family Meeting Room

Luc

"I still can't believe this has happened?" Isabell's aunt was as shaken as he was. She'd just been to the hospital room to see her niece. "I hadn't seen her in years, I just..."

"It's all right, ma'am." The counselor was there to speak with Luc and Sarah in the family meeting room at the hospital.

"Is it? Will it ever be all right? I wasn't there for her before."

"It's not your fault," Sally Ann said softly. She was the crisis counselor and had offered to sit with them to answer any questions.

They were all taken in. This woman needed help, but maybe it was a blessing in disguise. What happened to her was real, Dillon was plotting to murder her for her father's money.

"Is there any treatment for this disorder?" Luc asked pointedly.

"Well, the truth is, treatment for this delusional disorder is challenging, especially if the delusion this long lasting. Antipsychotic medications can be helpful, but delusions sometimes do not get better with pharmacological treatment. Since patients may not believe they have a mental disorder, they may refuse all treatment."

"Refuse treatment?"

"Yes, it's a possibility. Even psychotherapy."

"How can we can help her?"

"It may be possible to recover from psychosis without treatment, but that is the exception rather than the norm. Generally, untreated psychosis becomes worse over time. Psychosis like this one does not generally improve on its own."

"What exactly is this...disorder?" Sarah asked, fiddling with her coffee cup.

"Well, the definition is that a delusion is a false belief."

"A false belief?"

"Yes, one that is based on an incorrect interpretation of reality. A person with delusional disorder will firmly hold on to a false belief despite clear evidence to the contrary. Delusions can be caused by mental illnesses called psychoses."

"I see."

"Delusional disorder usually first affects people in middle or late adult life. It is less common than schizophrenia. Delusions may involve situations that could conceivably occur in real life, such as being followed, poisoned, infected, loved at a distance, or deceived by a spouse or lover."

"Really now?"

"Yes, there are different kinds of delusions. Delusions can be characterized as *persecutory,* such as belief that someone's going to be harmed by another person, group, or organization Or *grandiose* such as belief that the individual has exceptional abilities, wealth, or fame, or *erotomanic* such as a false belief that another individual is in love with him/her, and even *nihilistic* such as belief that a major catastrophe is about to happen. Because cognitive organization of the person are otherwise intact while in their delusional disorder, it's been described as a partial psychosis or non-bizarre psychosis."

"Non-bizarre?"

"Yes. Non-bizarre delusions are about situations that *could* occur in real life, such as being followed, being loved, having an infection, or even being deceived by one's spouse. Bizarre delusions are clearly implausible like being abducted by aliens.Some patients with delusional disorder don't have good insight into their pathological experiences since many of their other psychosocial abilities remain intact."

"I knew we had crazy folks in our family. I thought my brother was one, but this. This is too much." Sarah hugged her cup of coffee tightly.

"You'd be surprised, ma'am. The prevalence of delusional disorder in the United States is estimated to be around less than one per cent, while schizophrenia approximately one per cent and depressive disorders affect five per cent of the population."

"Unbelievable," Luc said.

"I wish she wasn't a statistic. I wish she wasn't too imaginative." Sarah shook her head while gripping her cup of coffee.

The counselor continued, "Well, having an imagination is not a bad thing in and of itself. Imagination is critical to society. The ability to imagine things pervades our entire existence. It influences everything we do, think about and create. Imagination has led to the creation of theories, dreams and inventions. Our ability to imagine, to come up with mental images and creative new ideas, is the result of something called a "mental workplace," a neural network that coordinates activity across multiple regions of the brain——that's why Isabell was able to draw from the novels and create her ideal man and bring him to life in her mind and in her world."

"Good God!" Sarah said.

"What causes Delusional Disorder?" Luc asked.

"As with many other psychotic disorders, the exact cause of delusional disorder isn't clear. Researchers are looking into genetic, biological, environmental and even psychological angles."

"I see."

"The fact that delusional disorder is more common in people who have family members with schizophrenia, it suggests a genetic angle. Researchers are studying how abnormalities in certain areas of the brain that control perception and thinking might be involved.

Evidence also suggests that delusional disorder can be triggered by stress."

"Can they ever fully recover?"

"It depends on the patient, the type of delusional disorder, and the person's life circumstances such as the availability of support and a willingness to stick with treatment. We'll do everything we can to help Isabell."

"Good to hear." He hesitated for a moment. "So stress brought this on?"

"In this case, yes. It looks that way."

What was going to happen to Isabell Morgan now?

EPILOGUE - ONE YEAR LATER

Ocean Bay Cove County Hospital
Isabell
"How are you feeling today, Ms. Morgan?" the nurse walked in with a bright smile and a tray with a silver cover.

Isabell sat up in the bed, breathing in a deep sigh. She was grateful to be alive. She was saddened to know that Erik and Courtney were resting peacefully in the back of her mind. A longing stabbed at her heart. But somehow through it all, she knew she was going to be fine. Everything was going to be all right. She was going to be discharged soon.

He was coming to pick her up. That was so nice of him. A true friend. He'd been checking up on her every day after work. The nurses told her that he wouldn't leave until he knew she was all right. He made sure she'd gotten the care she needed. All through it all, he'd been a good friend. Coming in after work, dropping by after a long shift.

"Feeling much better."

"Good. You'll be going home soon. Just thought I'd bring in your breakfast tray."

"Thank you."

She got up and put on her dressing gown. She went into the bathroom to brush her teeth and wash her face. She dried her face with the white towel. She fixed up her hair and brushed the kinks out.

She wasn't feeling alone anymore. Slowly, the loneliness was slipping away from her into the abyss. Was this what freedom felt like?

She was free from her demons, free from her fantasy, free from her delusions.

Or was she really?

Didn't we all pretend sometimes, maybe not to the extreme level, but wasn't dreaming beneficial to living? Dreams were as real as they lasted, as someone once said, could she say more of life?

She thought not.

Things were as real as we made them in our own minds. What was real to us may not be real to others.

When she was done getting dressed and shoving the last of her things into the suitcase, waiting for him to pick her up for her discharge, she thought of how long she'd travelled this past year. It had been quite a recovery.

Things could only get better, Isabell.

She sighed deeply.

She went to the table in the room and took the tray. The nurse had opened up the blinds in the room. Sunlight poured into the room. Was this an analogy for a bright future? Was this a good omen? Were things going to be different from now on?

People depended on each other. No man was an island, they said. And that was true, wasn't it? She never had any support, especially after her parents' murder, and her ex-boyfriend's abuse then her illness causing her to isolate everyone else in her life to where she'd invented people. Was it compensation for something that was so needed for human existence? Each other? People needed people to some degree - someone to love, and to be loved. Was that why the survival instinct in her conjured up the family she so desired to have?

A knock on the door distracted her thoughts.

"Good morning, beautiful," he said. A warm smile curved the corner of his lips. The smile touched his lovely eyes. He was such a kind, caring, and compassionate man. She felt his positive energy.

"Good morning, Detective Luc," she said.

"Hey, I thought we were on first name basis now."

"I said Luc, didn't I?" she teased him playfully.

He brought some more flowers for her. He'd brought flowers almost every week at the mental wellness ward and some teddy bears. Her favorite stuffed toys that reminded her of the happier times in her life.

"Not a detective anymore."

"What?"

"I quit the force a while back. I didn't want to mention it before. Yours was the last case."

"Oh no."

"Oh, it's nothing like that," he said, sensing her apprehension and guilt. "It was long overdue. I've always wanted to run my own detective agency. I'm thinking of taking some time off and figuring out what's important."

"Good move." She mellowed. He was such a good friend. She hoped it had nothing to do with the fact that he'd taken a personal interest in her case and even though his superiors were ready to write her off as the nutty professor, he'd taken up for her—defended her sanity, educated her about her condition. No one ever did that before.

"Thanks so much for picking me up."

"Hey, no worries. You need a ride to get home anyway."

A smile touched her lips. "I know," she said, quietly, "but you've picked me up in more than one way. Thank you, Luc."

"No worries." He shifted on the spot, hesitant at first. She'd never seen him that way before. He'd always been way cool and confident and smooth in his actions. "If you like, we could grab something to eat, besides...you know...hospital food," he said, looking at the tray with the slice of toast, hard boiled egg and Styrofoam cup of tea.

"I'd like that." Her voice was filled with emotion, overwhelming hope.

She reached over to hug him, his hug was firm and strong and reassuring. And for the first time in her life, she knew what true freedom felt like, she knew what happiness felt like.

About the author

Ann-Marie Richards has a degree in Psychology and enjoys reading and writing about matters pertaining to the human spirit. She loves to read mild psychological thrillers with a twist, powerful love stories, romance and mysteries. She is thrilled to hear from readers. You can send her an email at annmarierichards.author@gmail.com

CPSIA information can be obtained
at www.ICGtesting.com
Printed in the USA
BVHW070955271222
655041BV00008B/790